THE ROYAL HOUSE OF NIROLI

SEMPRE APPASSIONATA
SEMPRE REALE

Always passionate... Always regal

The richest royal dynasty in the world
– united by blood and passion, torn apart
by deceit and desire

THE OFFICIAL FIEREZZA FAMILY TREE

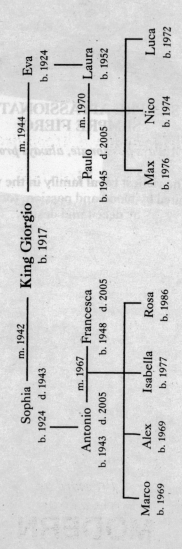

Sophia
b. 1924 d. 1943

m. 1942

King Giorgio
b. 1917

m. 1944

Eva
b. 1924

Antonio
b. 1943 d. 2005

m. 1967

Francesca
b. 1948 d. 2005

Paulo
b. 1945 d. 2005

m. 1970

Laura
b. 1952

Marco
b. 1969

Alex
b. 1969

Isabella
b. 1977

Rosa
b. 1986

Max
b. 1976

Nico
b. 1974

Luca
b. 1972

THE ROYAL HOUSE OF NIROLI

Bride by Royal Appointment

RAYE MORGAN

Presented by

MILLS & BOON®
MODERN™

*MILLS & BOON and MILLS & BOON with the Rose Device
are registered trademarks of the publisher.*

*First published in Great Britain 2008
by Harlequin Mills & Boon Limited, Eton House,
18-24 Paradise Road, Richmond, Surrey TW9 1SR*

Bride by Royal Appointment © Harlequin Books S.A. 2008

*Special thanks and acknowledgement are given to Raye Morgan
for her contribution to The Royal House of Niroli series.*

ISBN: 978 0 263 85878 5

52-0108

*Printed and bound in Spain
by Litografia Rosés S.A., Barcelona*

THE RULES OF
THE ROYAL HOUSE OF NIROLI

Rule 1: The ruler must be a moral leader. Any act which brings the Royal House into disrepute will rule a contender out of the succession to the throne.

Rule 2: No member of the Royal House may be joined in marriage without consent of the ruler. Any such union concluded results in exclusion and deprivation of honours and privileges.

Rule 3: No marriage is permitted if the interests of Niroli become compromised through the union.

Rule 4: It is not permitted for the ruler of Niroli to marry a person who has previously been divorced.

Rule 5: Marriage between members of the Royal House who are blood relations is forbidden.

Rule 6: The ruler directs the education of all members of the Royal House, even when the general care of the children belongs to their parents.

Rule 7: Without the approval or consent of the ruler, no member of the Royal House can make debts over the possibility of payment.

Rule 8: No member of the Royal House can accept inheritance nor any donation without the consent and approval of the ruler.

Rule 9: The ruler of Niroli must dedicate his life to the Kingdom. Therefore he is not permitted to have a profession.

Rule 10: Members of the Royal House must reside in Niroli or in a country approved by the ruler. However the ruler *must* reside in Niroli.

To CB, for friendship and sweet reason.
Thanks for being there!

CHAPTER ONE

THE kid was going to fall right over the edge.

Adam Ryder's anger at his son was barely leashed and he was fighting to hold it back. They'd come here for sightseeing, like all the other tourists strolling around them, but Adam wasn't thinking much about history as he climbed into the ruins of an ancient Roman villa on a site overlooking the Mediterranean Sea. The island of Niroli seemed to be crammed with castles and old crumbling walls and all sorts of antique relics but that wasn't what he'd come for.

Actually, he'd come to this particular location because it wasn't too far from the hotel and looked to be a good place to let his six-year old son, Jeremy, loose to run off some of the excess energy that was making him such a pain to be around.

But his reason for being on Niroli, a destination he'd avoided all his life? Ah, that was harder to explain.

Still, even he had to admit the island had a magic quality. He'd felt it right away as they'd stepped off the flight from New York. The air seemed softer. The sunlight

seemed to make things sparkle with possibilities. All of
which immediately made him wary. He couldn't let
things like that seduce him away from his goal.

After all, to put it plainly, he'd come to Niroli to do
a little fund-raising. He needed money to save his
company—big money—and he was willing to do
almost anything to get it, including accepting an unusual
offer that had been made to him—the crown of this
little island country. And there was nothing magical
about that.

Meanwhile, he had to deal with Jeremy. He'd brought
the boy along hoping to create a few bonding opportunities, but his interest in that project was waning fast.
The thing was, the nanny he'd hired to come along and
take care of his son had quit right there in the airport,
loudly declaring she couldn't stand the boy just
moments before boarding the plane.

Adam kept remembering the odd, slightly triumphant
smile on Jeremy's face as she had stormed away. He'd
faced off grown men in bar fights in his younger days
with hardly a quiver of fear, but the look on his son's
face, just before departing all known civilization with
only him in tow, still sent shivers down his spine. He
knew how to handle adults, both male and female. But
what was he going to do with this kid?

"Take him out and let him run," the woman at the
concierge desk at the hotel had suggested.

So here he was, letting Jeremy run. And the boy certainly ran. Up and down and all over the ruins, his blond
hair flying in the breeze. At least he seemed interested in

the ruins. That was something. He'd spent the entire plane ride asking, "Are we there yet?" until Adam had had to bite down on his own hand to keep from yelling at him.

Now Jeremy was balancing on the viaduct that had once brought water to the villa, a portion of which came perilously close to the edge of the cliff. Adam frowned. He supposed he should do the parental thing and warn him about falling.

"Jeremy, don't go out on the edge like that," he called out. "It's dangerous."

The boy looked back at him and laughed. Adam shook his head. What six-year-old boy laughed like that, with that wicked tone, as though he relished torturing adults? The only thing he could think was that he'd better hire another, tougher nanny, and do it fast.

"Stay away from the edge."

Jeremy turned from the viaduct, but he began to climb the crumbling exterior wall of the old villa instead. Adam started toward him. This was getting ridiculous. The kid was going to kill himself.

"Jeremy! Damn it, get down from there right now!"

Jeremy turned to climb higher—and fell right over the edge.

The shout that came from Adam seemed to rip through the walls of his chest. Shock and then sharp fear jolted through him and he began to run, cursing and praying at the same time. Oh, God! What if…?

He threw himself into the ruin and began to scramble up the steep wall, heading for the spot where Jeremy had gone over the edge. The Roman bricks crumbled under his feet, making for impossible climbing, but then he gained the harder ledge and vaulted up into position. Looking down, he braced himself for the sight of his son's shattered body lying on the rocks, thirty feet below.

Instead, he saw Jeremy kneeling at the feet of a slender woman, petting what looked like a golden retriever, and from his new vantage point he could see that there was a shelf, a sort of patio area, that jutted out over the sea, not far beneath him.

He took a deep breath and let his shoulders sag, but relief was followed quickly by raw anger. Now he realized that Jeremy hadn't fallen. He'd jumped. Adam let out an angry shout, then turned and made his way to the stone steps he noticed along the side. By the time he reached where the young woman was sitting on an old stone wall, Jeremy and the dog had gone on down to the rocky shore beneath and were now frolicking at the water's edge.

His anger at his son was only made worse by his sense of frustration, and he swore, then turned grudgingly toward the woman.

"Sorry," he muttered, just in case she was the type to take offense.

And then he stopped and looked again. She was quite striking. Her body was slim and graceful, her dark brown hair sleek and shining in the sunlight and braided with a silk scarf the color of spring leaves. Her neck seemed unusually long and slender, making him think of ballet dancers. He couldn't see her eyes as she wore a pair of very dark and stylish Gucci sunglasses, but the features he could see could have been classically cut in fine porcelain. In direct contrast, her mouth was full and lush and sensual, and her chin tilted impudently.

"I hope my son didn't bother you," he said, his gaze sliding over the creamy skin of her bare arms.

Her blouse was lacy, her skirt a wide swath of emerald-green gauze. Her feet looked delicate in leather sandals, the toenails painted a pearly pink. There was an elf-like air of the forest sprite about her, though she was too tall and well rounded to be a fairy. Altogether, she was very much the most enchanting creature he'd seen in a long time. He turned toward her the way plants responded to sunlight—as though he had to have her in his life.

"Oh, no," she responded pleasantly. "I enjoyed meeting him. He seems like a wonderful boy."

"Wonderful? Hah." That almost startled a laugh from him, but he liked her musical speaking voice with its faint accent adding a certain lilting charm. "I guess you didn't really have time to get to know him," he noted dryly.

A frown appeared between her neat eyebrows. "Is that supposed to be a joke?" she asked bluntly. "Why would you say such a thing about your own son?"

He hesitated. It probably did sound cold to someone who hadn't been thoroughly annoyed by Jeremy yet. He had a pang of remorse. Maybe she was right and he was getting too cynical about the boy.

"Frustration, I guess," he said, rubbing a hand through his sand-colored hair and giving her the up-from-under-his-eyebrows look that had been known to make grown women swoon like teenagers. "It's been a long, wearing day."

She didn't swoon. In fact, her mouth thinned a bit. "Oh?" she said in a tone that bespoke impending boredom. It was obvious she hadn't been charmed.

"We just flew in from New York," he explained.

"I see."

She turned her face and looked out over the ocean. He was feeling dismissed. That surprised him. In his Hollywood milieu he was considered a very attractive, not to mention very powerful, man. The production company he'd founded and ran to this day was one of the most important in the business, despite the takeover nightmare it was going through right now.

And beside that, he didn't suffer dismissal lightly. If there was any dismissing to be done, he liked to be the one doing it. An impulse to confront her reaction rose in him right away.

But he fought it. For once he wasn't getting the admiring female response he was used to taking as his due. So what? He had more important things to take care of.

Looking down at the shoreline, he saw that Jeremy was still playing with the dog. He supposed he should go down and join them. But at that moment, the dog shook water from his wet fur all over Jeremy, and Adam grimaced.

Between rolling in the wet sand with a boy and a dog and hanging around on the ledge trying to get a beautiful woman to admit he was worth getting to know, the choice was an easy one. It was the challenge, he told himself. He glanced at the stone wall she was sitting on.

"Mind if I join you?" he asked, moving to do just that without waiting for her answer.

She hesitated just long enough to let him know this wasn't her preference, but she was polite.

"Please do," she said coolly, but she was gracious, shifting a little to be sure there was room for him and moving a huge canvas bag that looked big enough to contain all her earthly possessions.

He sat close enough to get a hint of her scent. It was fresh and spicy and not very sweet. For some reason, that gave him a frisson of excitement for just a moment, and immediately he was flooded with an urge to kiss those full lips.

He drew himself up, startled. He hadn't reacted so viscerally to a woman in years—and he was used to being around a lot of beautiful women. Maybe it was the magic of the place, the soft, seductive breeze, the sound of the gentle waves on the beach below. He turned quickly, looking out at the ocean, thrown off a bit and not sure whether he wanted her to see how he was responding to her or not. If there was one thing he hated it was revealing any sort of vulnerability.

And that was a reaction he was noticing in himself more and more lately. He didn't trust anyone much, but experience had taught him that beautiful women were the most likely to betray you in a purely personal way.

What was the expression? Once bitten, twice shy? He'd been bitten all right. He'd practically had his arm chewed off a few times. And, yeah, he was shy. Damn shy. He was going to require big-time proof before he could be convinced trust was worth the cost.

Still, that didn't mean he didn't enjoy the game. He just didn't expect to win any prizes or take home the game pieces when he won.

"Nice view," he said gruffly, looking out over the huge expanse of sparkling Mediterranean water. "Do you come here often?"

"All the time. It's my favorite place to come when I have big decisions to make," she told him candidly. "Or when I feel the need to get away from it all."

Turning toward him, she smiled and her small white teeth gleamed in the golden sunlight. "Or when I just want to commune with my ancient ancestors."

"Ancestors, huh?"

He smiled back at her, ready to flirt if she was going loosen up a bit. Flirting didn't cost much. You didn't have to lay yourself open for it to work, and it could be fun. It could also lead to some quality bed time. You just never did know. And she was the most appealing potential bed partner he'd seen in a long, long time. It might be worth wading through her prickly attitude to get to the good stuff.

"This place is crawling with my ancestors," she said, waving a hand in the air as though there were groups of them hanging around all up and down the cliffs and caves.

"No kidding?" He looked around at the rock wall behind them, willing to join in her conceit if she would let him play. "Why don't you introduce me?"

She laughed softly. "What do you care about my musty old Nirolian ancestors?"

"You'd be surprised. I've got a few of my own."

She cocked a sleek eyebrow. "Do you?"

"So they tell me."

At last there was a spark of interest in her manner. He supposed she'd be even more interested if he told her he was King Giorgio of Niroli's illegitimate grandson.

But it had never been a point of pride with him. In fact, he'd been raised with the vague feeling that it was really something to be ashamed of. There was no doubt that his maternal grandparents thought it was something his *mother* should be ashamed of. But then, they had always thought just about everything his mother did should be hushed up. And since they'd pretty much raised him on their Kansas farm, it was an attitude that lingered stubbornly in his psyche, no matter how hard he tried to deny it.

"But I thought you just came from New York," the graceful woman was saying.

"That's right. I've never been here to Niroli before. But my father was...Nirolian."

"Ah."

She stretched the syllable out as though that explained everything—and not in a good way. He frowned. Her attitude was beginning to get on his nerves. But before he could probe it further, Jeremy shrieked and the dog barked. He rose, looking down to see what was going on.

"Jeremy, leave that dog alone," he called down. He

didn't know if his son had actually done anything to the animal, but he thought he might as well cover all bases.

"His name is Fabio," she said coolly.

"Who? Oh, the dog?"

"Yes."

"Okay." He turned and called down again. "Jeremy, leave Fabio alone."

"You aren't very good at it, are you?" she said dryly as he sat down again.

He looked at her, startled. "At what?"

"Parenting. You don't seem to have the knack for it."

He stared at her. Now he was sure of it. She hated him. What right did she have to decide to hate him at first sight anyway? He was a decent guy. And she was damn annoying.

"What do you know about my parenting skills?"

"I can hear it in the way you talk to him. You shouldn't talk to a boy that age the way you do. You can't order him about as though he were a soldier."

He couldn't believe this. She actually thought she could tell him how to raise his kid. "He needs some discipline," he said, pointing out what was obvious to the rest of the world.

"Why aren't you disciplining him, then?"

He stared at her. Was she purposefully goading him? "That's what I'm trying to do!"

She shook her head. "There you go, raising your voice again."

And he thought he'd been frustrated before? "What do you prefer?" he shot back, making a Herculean effort not to let his voice get harsher. "Do you think I should hit him?"

"Of course not. I think you should give him some structure." She sighed. "I'll bet you don't know him very well, no matter how often you have him around."

She turned toward him in that odd way she had. He wished she would take off those dark glasses so he could read more in her eyes.

"But it's not often, is it? And you came to Niroli thinking you could get closer to your son just by being here with him."

She had certainly hit the nail on the head with that guess. In fact, she seemed almost eerily clairvoyant. But he hated to admit she was right about anything. "What if I did?"

She shrugged her slender shoulders. "Well, I don't think it's working. And if you don't improve your technique, it's not going to work, no matter how loud you get." She looked at him with pity. "You need help."

He stifled the angry answer that sprang to his lips. She was just plain wrong, but arguing about it wasn't going to get him anywhere. "Okay," he said instead, opting with difficulty for sweet reason—giving charm one last chance to make a difference. "Help me, then."

Her smile was meant as a reaction and not a way to draw him in. "I think not."

Her superior tone was maddening. She was dismissing him again. Well, if she was such a damn expert...

"So how many children do *you* have?" he asked pointedly.

She raised her head, amused at how angry he was getting, and at how hard he was trying to hide it.

"Not one." She said it without a hint of embarrassment. "I don't even have a husband at this point."

"Then why the hell should I listen to you?"

She tossed her head. "You'd better listen to someone. Your intuition doesn't seem to be doing you any good at all."

There, Elena Valerio thought coolly. *That ought to do it.* Now he would get up and storm off and she would be rid of him. And that was exactly what she wanted… wasn't it?

She wished she could see him. That didn't happen often these days. She'd accepted her blindness years ago and she had worked out so many ways to compensate, she almost felt it an advantage at times. But from the first, his brusque voice and his cocky manner had triggered something in her she couldn't explain, and she wished she could put a face to the image she was getting.

She heard impatience and a world-weary cynicism that she didn't like. He was a user—that was what she heard. His arrogance was only exceeded by his need to control those around him. At the same time he seemed to want to charm her, she sensed a strange coldness inside him that chilled her. He was everything she disliked in a man.

But he was still here. What was he waiting for? She sighed.

"Okay, mister. Here's a free tip. Relax."

"Relax? Why should I relax?"

"Didn't you come to Niroli to refresh yourself?"

"No. I came on business."

"Ah, that explains it. You should let that tension go. It's tying you in knots. Your son can sense that, so he doesn't trust you. It's no wonder he defies you."

Adam bit his tongue to keep from giving back to her as good as he was getting. He was sure there were a few home truths he could aim in her direction if he gave it some thought. But that would get them nowhere. He decided to take a new tack instead.

"You have beautiful hair," he said, looking at how it gleamed in the sunlight and resisting the urge to reach out and touch it.

"Do I?" She seemed surprised. "I must say I like the way it feels on my back." She swished it against the skin exposed by the low-cut blouse.

"You have a beautiful back, too," he added for good measure.

She stiffened. "That's getting a little personal, don't you think?"

"Sorry," he said unconvincingly.

"No, you're not."

He'd just about had it with her. "Would you explain why you took an instant dislike to me?" he asked.

"Does it come through that clearly?" She pressed her lips together, then smiled. "Good."

He stared at her. He knew he should get up and leave. She didn't want him here. And yet, he couldn't seem to tear himself away. He wanted her to like him. Or maybe he just wanted her to admit he wasn't that bad so he could be the one to dismiss *her*. He wasn't sure which it was.

"Maybe I can explain my…less-than-friendly re-action to you this way. You think women should fall for you like…like apples in a tree, right into your arms. Don't you?"

"So what are you saying?" he quipped back. "That you're not ripe yet?"

She gave him a baleful look from behind the glasses.

"Or maybe, it's this. That you're forbidden fruit?"

She couldn't help but laugh at that one. "Bingo," she said, then sobered. "Now if you don't mind…"

"But I do mind." He breathed in her scent again and knew that was part of the reason he didn't want to leave her. She smelled like exotic fruit—forbidden or not. And he was rapidly developing a taste for it. He stayed right where he was and began to talk about simple, banal things around them, just to try to lower the unease between them.

Listening to him, Elena began to tap her foot ner-vously. He put her on edge and she didn't like that. She came to this place for peace and resuscitation, not to be the object of a verbal joust.

She wondered for a moment if she should call Fabio back. She'd been told when he first came to work for her that she wasn't to let him play with children. He was a professional with tasks to perform and it would confuse him to treat him like a house pet. At first she'd been very rigid about it, making sure he toed the line in all aspects of their relationship. But the more she'd grown to depend upon him, the more she'd relaxed. He was enjoying the boy. She could hear them both. That told her he was still close enough so that she didn't need to worry. And they were having such a good time. She smiled. She would let him play awhile longer.

The man's arm brushed hers and she almost gasped. Luckily, she controlled the impulse, but she bit into her lower lip to do it. He didn't seem to notice. He was talking about the sunlight on the ocean and the quality of the water below them. Ordinary things. Things anyone might talk about. And though he hadn't left, he wasn't being so obnoxious anymore. She sighed. Maybe he wasn't so bad. She shouldn't be so judgmental. He was probably a decent enough fellow.

And yet…

There was something there that bothered her, something she could hear in his voice. An underlying unhappiness, perhaps—an old wound that still festered. Something that ate at him deep inside.

But she had no intention of trying to help this man. He wasn't a friend and he was never going to be. She moved impatiently, about to call Fabio back to her side, but her foot struck the side of her canvas bag and she felt it overturn and spill its contents onto the ground.

"Oh, bother," she muttered, leaning down to collect her belongings.

But he did it for her. "Here you go," he said, but then he hesitated and she waited, wondering what he'd found that interested him among her things.

"So you're an artist," he said at last.

She frowned, surprised. "Of sorts," she replied, thinking of her musicianship. She'd been extremely musical from the beginning, and once she'd lost her sight, at age four, she'd plunged into music as a way of communicating with a world that didn't know what to do with people like her. "How did you know?"

"I can see you've been sketching."

She went very still. What on earth was the man talking about? "Have I?" she said carefully.

"Yes. Here's your sketchbook. It fell out of your bag."

My sketchbook? What sketchbook?

Then her mind cleared. Ah, Gino. Her very gay, very artistic friend who often came along when she climbed out here in the ruins. He'd come along today, but had gone back to the house to make a phone call. The sketchbook had to be his.

"Mind if I look at these?" the man was asking.

"Oh, why not?" She laughed softly, wondering what else Gino had left in her bag.

She heard pages rustling, but there was dead silence from her companion.

"Wow," he said at last, his voice somewhat strangled. "Michelangelo's got nothing on you."

She frowned, wondering what on earth that meant. "It's nice to have one's work appreciated," she said ambiguously.

"You do have a way with…" he cleared his throat "…uh, the nude male form."

She choked back a laugh. *Oh, Gino, what have you been up to?* From the nuances she sensed in this man's voice, whatever he'd found on the pages was pretty darn provocative. She could just imagine—Gino unleashed!

Good heavens. And just how did he suppose that a blind woman managed that sort of thing? But he still didn't realize she was blind. People often didn't catch on at first. She'd trained herself to move and express herself just as a sighted person would. Fate had played a very large, serious joke on her and she enjoyed playing her little joke on the world in return. Still, most people got clued in relatively quickly. Usually seeing her with Fabio and putting two and two together was what did it. But then, he hadn't really seen her with her dog, had he? He'd seen his son with Fabio, not her, and the connection hadn't been made. Interesting.

"So you like the style?" she asked, having a hard time holding back a chuckle. "Tell me. Which is your favorite?"

He choked for just a moment, and his voice was a bit ragged when he responded. "Why don't you tell me which is yours?"

"Hmm." She put her head to the side. "I think I love them all."

"Right." He drew in a sharp breath and didn't seem to have a good response to that one.

He didn't know what to make of her. It was obvious. Finding nude sketches in her bag presented a whole new side of her from his point of view. He was probably trying to decide whether to take it as an earthy invitation to intimacy—or to run for cover. The laughter bubble was coming up her throat and she didn't know how long she would be able to hold it back.

"So… Do you hire models for this kind of thing?" he asked carefully.

She shook her head. She knew it was time to stop this. She could hear the intensity building in his voice. The thought of her sketching these nude male images was turning him on in a big way. And an aroused, aggressive man whom she didn't really know was something she didn't want to deal with. But she couldn't resist one last needling.

"Why? Are you offering your services?" She raised an eyebrow and waited to see what he would say.

"That would depend on the compensation," he said, moving closer, his voice deepening.

She moved a little away, but still asked, "What would you consider a fair price?"

He paused, and for some reason her pulse began to quicken.

"I always say the kindness of a beautiful woman is worth more than gold."

His voice was low and seductive now and he was moving even closer to her. If his son hadn't been romping nearby, she was sure he would have made some sort of move by now. Surprisingly, she felt a quick shiver of apprehension. The joke was played out. She had let this go on too long as it was. Once again, as her friends always warned her, she was playing with fire and she was going to get burned if she didn't put out the flames right away.

CHAPTER TWO

"I've never been one to trust much in "the kindness of strangers"," Elena said quickly, lifting her chin and making sure any hint of teasing was erased from her tone. Instead, she was back to being brisk and dismissive. "And I'm not hiring right now. In fact, if you don't mind…"

Her words stopped in her throat. He'd leaned very close to her, so close she could feel his warm breath on her cheek.

"But I do mind, beautiful lady," he said, his voice very quiet, but hard as steel. "And I don't like being played with."

He didn't touch her, but she felt as though he had. Suddenly she was breathless and her heart was hammering in her chest. She wasn't sure if it was from fear or excitement. Either way, it was something she wasn't used to. And she wanted it to stop. Had she gone too far this time? Had she walked too close to the edge?

But in the next second, all was confusion as a crowd of tourists appeared on the ruin above the terrace, and Fabio was back, panting happily and pushing his head against her knee, and she sensed the man drawing away. And then he was calling his son and she heard the crunch of crumbled stone in his departure.

On pure reflex, her hand rose and covered the area of her face where his warm breath had seared it. His voice and the sense of his presence had disturbed something in her in a way she'd never felt before. She shivered and hoped fervently she would never come across the man again.

"Hey, are you all right?"

Gino was back. She sighed and smiled at him in relief.

"I'm fine," she lied, then shivered one last time. "But I think one of my ancestors just walked across my grave."

"Elena Valerio, you are in big trouble."

She moaned softly and made a face as she settled back into her chair at the trendy sidewalk café she frequented every morning. She was talking to herself in public again. She had to nip this new bad habit in the bud. People would think she was going mad. Even Fabio had lifted his head questioningly. She could sense it.

"You know you're in trouble when even your dog turns on you," she murmured, scratching him behind the ears.

And so she was, though it had nothing to do with Fabio at all. Her trouble was all about a restlessness that had come over her since meeting the child Jeremy and his disturbing father the day before. She felt as though she'd been sleepwalking, living life in a daze, and now, suddenly, the man she'd met had shaken her awake. Awakening was painful. She had to face the fact that she'd been letting herself drift. If she didn't pull herself together and begin to take charge of her life, she was going to hit the rocks.

Elena had lived in Niroli all her life, and that life had been pleasant and peaceful despite her disability. She'd been raised by her grandmother in a small cottage here in the sleepy town of Monte Speziare, where the old ways were treasured and the new tourist hotels and other developments to the south were looked upon with horror. Her grandmother had recently died, leaving nothing but the little cottage they lived in, and Elena was supporting herself by giving piano lessons and hoping to scrape together enough money to attend a special music therapy training program in New York.

At least, that was what she told herself. And yet, she'd just found out that morning that one of her best students was leaving for Italy. That left her with hardly enough daily fees coming in to feed herself, much less prepare for any sort of future. It was definitely time to start getting serious about things. She needed new revenue.

And she needed to stop thinking about men. Well, not *men*, actually. One man. One man who had shaken up her emotions at the same time he'd shaken her assumptions. It was strange the way he'd tangled himself into her thoughts. She didn't like him and yet she couldn't stop thinking about him.

Suddenly, she felt prickles on the back of her neck. "Oh, no," she whispered. She didn't need to see him. She could feel him. He was coming toward her and there was nothing she could do to avoid him.

Well, at least this was a completely public place. Maybe things would go better here. He couldn't try to intimidate her.

Better yet, maybe they would pass without seeing her. She tried to make herself small in her chair, turned her face toward the stucco wall of the café, held her breath.

And then she heard a familiar voice.

"Hey! Look! It's Fabio. Come on!"

"Jeremy!"

She slumped in her chair. It would seem that things were just going to get more and more complicated. There was no way out.

Adam saw her at the same time Jeremy did, and he tried, too late, to steer his son toward the other side of the road. Jeremy ran straight for the little street-side café where she was sipping a drink and he followed, reluctantly. The last thing in the world he needed was another run-in with the aggravating lady in the Gucci shades.

He had enough on his mind. He'd barely been in Niroli twenty-four hours and already he was itching to leave. Jeremy was driving him crazy and his first meeting with the counselors at the palace had been less than reassuring. He'd expected to show up, meet his grandfather, King Giorgio, maybe have a lot of people make a big fuss over how glad they were to see him, and then come away with a contract to look over, options to weigh. That was the way things were done in the real world, weren't they? It should have been cut and dried.

Instead, he'd been received as though no one was

quite sure who he was or why he was there wasting their time. He'd been shuffled from one room to another until he'd finally ended up talking to a dour man named Tours who had claimed they'd thought he wasn't coming until the next week. The truth had finally come out—the royal counselors in charge of this thing were off on holiday and now they expected him to cool his heels until they came back.

He didn't have time for that. His company was undergoing a hostile takeover back in California. He needed resolution and he needed money and he needed both fast. Strong words had ensued. Thinking back, he realized that hadn't helped matters. He was going to have to work on controlling his temper. They didn't seem to know how to react to it.

Tours had then insisted he transfer from his hotel to rooms in the palace, all the better, no doubt, to keep tabs on him. Adam had insisted he would do no such thing. If he had to wait around for a week, at least he was going to do it on his own terms.

And when he had asked to see his grandfather, Tours had acted as though he had to prove himself worthy first. But why should that surprise him? Had he really imagined they were going to welcome him with open arms, his illegitimacy forgiven? More fool he. It was more than evident that the situation of his birth was a big issue, and that there were factions who were opposed to him being offered the job in the first place. This had certainly turned out to be more complicated than he had been led to believe.

What was the big deal, anyway? All they wanted was to hire a king for their little island country. He'd put together multimillion-dollar international projects with fewer hassles than this looked as if it was going to take.

In the meantime, he couldn't get hold of anyone back in Hollywood and he needed to make sure some dotting of i's and crossing of t's was going on in his absence. He was also going to have to warn Zeb Vargas, his number two at Ryder Productions, that this was going to take more time than he'd thought it would. Deals were hanging in the balance. Banks were waiting for authorizations. Writers and actors he wanted under contract were being enticed away by other producers with more ready cash. Profits were melting away in the sun. He needed to get things settled.

And so he approached the beautiful lady without a smile, nodding shortly and grunting a greeting, while Jeremy wrapped his arms around the dog's neck and murmured unintelligible love to the animal, who accepted it all with happy panting.

"Hello," she said, turning slightly toward him and then away again. "What a surprise. I didn't think we'd ever meet up again." She frowned slightly. "This is a bit off the beaten tourist path. Are you staying nearby?"

That was another problem. The press had already sniffed out his hotel accommodations and for that reason—and other, having to do with Jeremy—he was in the market for a new place to stay. Nothing seemed as simple as it should be in this little country.

"Not for long," he said gruffly, wondering why she

didn't look at him. Memories of their last meeting came back to him and he felt a vague sense of irritation. She could at least pretend not to hate him.

"Can I take Fabio for a walk?" Jeremy interrupted eagerly.

Elena hesitated, obviously reluctant to extend the meeting. Adam picked up on that and shared her impulse.

"Uh, I think we have to get going," he began, but his son's intensity drowned out his words.

"Oh, please, please!" Jeremy cried, with Fabio happily licking his face. "He's my best friend now."

Adam looked at his son in astonishment. He'd never heard that childlike pleading tone from him before. Usually it was all demands and whining. There seemed to be something special in Jeremy's relationship to this pair. Odd.

"Well, just for a moment," Elena was saying, and he knew it was reluctantly. "I'll tell you what you can do. Do you see a butcher's shop down the street a bit?"

"Yes. The one with the hanging sign?"

"That's the one. If you take Fabio to the back door of that shop, I think the butcher will give him a bone. He often does. Just knock on the door."

"Great," Jeremy said, jumping up and brimming with joy.

"Wait a minute," she added. "He has his harness on today. You must hold it from the top, like this." She demonstrated and Jeremy took over, racing off with his new best friend.

Adam watched them go, dodging the few people

who strolled up and down the charming street, window-shopping in the tiny shops along the way. He was still impressed by how different Jeremy could be when he wanted to.

"That's quite a rig you have on the dog," he noted in passing. "It looks almost like…"

He stopped dead, looking at her quickly. *Almost like the kind the blind use*, he'd been about to say. And suddenly it hit him. The moment he realized the truth, he felt as though he'd been smacked in the solar plexus with a football.

"Yes, he is a guide dog," she said calmly. "And, yes, I am. Blind, that is."

He was still too stunned to speak, not to mention the accompanying humiliation of being such a fool as not to have noticed before.

"Oh, pick your jaw up off the ground," she said briskly.

"I…I'm so sorry, I…"

"No need to be sorry. It's been quite amusing. I threw all kinds of hints out there that you didn't pick up on." She smiled serenely. "I think you hold the record. You're the most clueless man I've ever met."

"I… listen, I just didn't…"

"It's been almost a good twenty-four hours, hasn't it? I once went three hours straight with an elderly man with a hearing problem who didn't realize I was blind, but he was talking at the top of his lungs the whole time. And at ninety-four you expect a little density. But you!" She grinned, happy to have found a vulnerability in him. "You take the prize."

He knew he was flushing. Luckily, she couldn't see that, could she? Now if he could just get a steady tone back in his voice, he might be able to get back in control of this situation. He sank into a chair across from where she was sitting and looked at her, hard.

She was blind. For some reason that tore at him in a way he wasn't prepared for. What a tragedy. She was so beautiful. His compassion for her hardship actually overwhelmed his resentment for having been fooled—and that wasn't like him.

A waiter appeared, offered coffee drinks, and retreated again, and Adam nodded his response, but his mind was completely engaged in this lovely woman's situation.

"My son says your name is Elena," he managed to say at last, leaning forward and talking very slowly.

"Yes. Elena Valerio."

"I am Adam Ryder," he went on gingerly. "And I guess you've picked up that my son is Jeremy."

She groaned, letting her head fall back. "Mr Ryder, I'm blind, not deaf, not hard of hearing, or even somewhat slow. You don't have to speak carefully to me. Please. Just use your normal voice."

He flushed again, annoyed at…what? Being caught out trying to be compassionate? That was the problem. It didn't come naturally to him. No wonder she'd nailed him on it.

"Okay, Elena Valerio," he said, speaking in a quick staccato. "I'm Adam. And if you skip the jokes about the Garden of Eden, I'll lay off treating you like you're in need of a keeper."

Smiling, she stuck out a slender hand. "You've got a deal. It's nice to meet you, Adam Ryder."

He took her hand in his and held it a moment too long, studying it, admiring the long, slender fingers, the pink nails, the smooth skin.

"It's nice of you to say so, Elena Valerio," he responded as she pulled her hand away again. "I hope nothing happens to make you change your mind."

She looked startled. "What could happen? Why are you talking in riddles?"

He smiled, glad to be back in control. "Tired of games? You seemed all for them yesterday."

It was her turn to flush. "Sorry about that," she said breezily. "But you've got to admit, you asked for it."

He wasn't prepared to admit anything of the kind, but he didn't say so. He was still trying to adjust to the fact of her blindness. There were so many angles to it, aspects he'd never considered before. He pushed away the pity factor immediately. His intuition told him she would scorn any sort of sympathy for her condition. And that left him to wonder at her elegance and how gracefully she seemed to deal with the situation. He couldn't imagine coming to terms with such a thing himself. Anger and bitterness would probably rule his life.

As if they didn't already, he thought wryly, though he knew he was overstating a bit. Still, no one would call him a happy man these days. A cynical man, yes. A hard man. Life tended to make you that way.

He'd been taken aback recently when he'd overheard

a young female employee at his film production company say, "Mr Ryder is so hot. How come he never smiles?"

Smile, he'd thought at the time. What the hell was there to smile about, anyway? Who had time? Smiling was for losers.

And yet he'd made it a point to stop by the men's room and look into a mirror. She was right. Smiling didn't seem to come naturally anymore. He finally forced the corners of his mouth up into the proper shape but his silver-blue eyes didn't join in. They were still as cold as an Arctic winter.

He hadn't been born angry. In fact, despite having a mother who spent her days dashing about the world with the jet set, his childhood had been relatively calm. But it seemed as if he was angry all the time lately. Maybe that was why Jeremy was so impossible to handle. The sins of the father and all that.

He looked at Elena and wondered if she had a lover.

"I guess you didn't make those sketches, did you?" he said sadly.

Her laugh sounded like chimes. "No, I did not."

"That's disappointing."

"Such a pity." She pretended sympathy. "You thought you'd found a woman with a lot of naked male anatomy on her mind."

She had him there. The idea had been appealing. "I thought I'd found a very interesting woman, that's for sure."

"So women aren't interesting if there is no sex involved?"

There was a pause, and then he said softly, just because he couldn't resist, "Who says there's no sex involved?"

"I..."

That stopped her for the moment. She actually blushed. He grinned. The waiter brought a tall coffee drink he didn't recognize as anything he would have ever ordered, but he accepted it, then waited for the man to leave before he leaned forward and asked, "So if you didn't draw them, who did?"

"My friend Gino did. He came out on the ruins with me, but he went back before you arrived to make a phone call and left his sketchbook in my bag."

That made him raise his eyebrows. "So he's the one interested in male nudes."

She smiled. "You might say that. He's a very good artist, isn't he?"

"I suppose. Though I'd be a better judge of that if the nudes were female."

Her smile faded. She didn't need any reminders that he was aggressively heterosexual. His vibes were coming through loud and clear—and making her nervous. She had no intention of getting chummy. As soon as Fabio and the boy came back, she would find an excuse to leave. In the meantime, she didn't mind sparring with him a bit, as long as he didn't take it as an invitation toward anything friendlier.

He moved and she tensed, not sure what he was going to do, then felt a bit foolish when it was obvious he was just using his cell phone. She reached for her drink, as if that had been her objective all along, but she knew she wasn't fooling anyone.

"Damn," he said after a moment. "Why don't cell phones work around here? I can't get through to anyone on this phone."

"Is it set up for international?" she asked.

"I bought it deliberately for just that reason," he said. "I'm beginning to wonder if there's a magic button or something."

It was on the tip of her tongue to offer him the use of her landline. Her cottage was just around the corner. But she stopped herself just in time. She really didn't want this man in her little house. Better not to suggest it. There ought to be a line he could use at whatever hotel he was checked into.

"Where are you staying?" she asked, since the subject had come up, at least in her mind.

"Why do you want to know?" he shot back without missing a beat.

"Oh!" This was surely the most defensive and distrustful man she'd ever met. She made a quick sound of exasperation. "What do you mean, why do I want to know? That is so rude!"

"Sorry," he said gruffly. "But, believe me, I have reason to not want people to know where I'm staying." He hesitated. "We started out at the Ritz but I'm afraid we've got to move to another place. They've likely put our possessions in the street by now."

She shook her head, uncomprehending. "What are you talking about? What happened?"

He sighed heavily. "My adorable son Jeremy happened. As usual."

She frowned. The man was impossible. "I wish you wouldn't talk about him that way."

"*I* wish I didn't have to." He saw the look on her face and backed down a bit. "Okay, I'll try to hold back on the sarcasm. But, believe me, you'll be saying mean things about him too when you hear what he did."

She made a disbelieving face. "Tell me."

He took a sip of his unfamiliar coffee drink and had to admit it was pretty good. Settling back, he began his story.

"Here's how it all went down. I was up half the night trying to make business calls to the States, so Jeremy woke up before I did this morning and headed out to see whose life he could ruin."

"Adam!"

He grinned, then, realizing she couldn't see a grin, shrugged and went on. "When I woke up and saw he was gone, I knew right away we were in trouble. I searched all over for him, looking for evidence of recent disasters. It took awhile, but I finally went to the hotel kitchen. And there he was."

"And? What did he do there—sneak a cookie?"

"Oh, no." He issued a short laugh. "Jeremy never does small things like that. I'll tell you what he did." He grimaced, remembering the sight he was about to recount to her. "You see, the kitchen staff were preparing for a wedding, and in a sweetly fashioned little portico they had placed a beautifully decorated wedding cake, all ready to go. It was about five layers tall. And

I'm sure it was a work of art…before Jeremy got to it
and licked off most of the frosting."

She gasped. "Oh, no!"

"Oh, yes." He groaned, stretching out in his chair
and shaking his head as he remembered the horrible
scene. "The funny thing was, he liked the yellow roses
and gobbled them right down, but the red roses didn't
taste right to him, so as he pulled them off he merely
squished them on the table. They looked like sad little
soldiers lying there, abused and unwanted. It was heart-
breaking. Really."

Elena was trying not to laugh but it wasn't easy
holding it back.

"In the meantime, he dipped his finger into the white
foundation coat, making swirly pictures as he scooped
off hunks of white frosting and gorged himself with it.
And no one caught him in time, so he just kept eating.
He was looking a bit green around the gills by the time
I found him—and still trying to stuff more frosting
down his greedy gullet."

She sighed, shaking her head. "Poor Jeremy."

"Poor Jeremy?" He was slightly outraged by her mis-
directed sympathy. "How about poor Jeremy's father?
Or the poor pastry chef? Or the poor bride, for God's
sake. You should have heard the screaming once
everyone realized what had happened."

She held back a chuckle. "What did you do?"

He shrugged. "I threw some money at them and
grabbed the kid and got out of there. Believe me, I don't
think we should go back. We've been wandering the

streets ever since." He sighed. "So now we have to find a new place to stay. Then I'll send for our clothes."

He threw some money at them. She nodded silently, thinking that was probably what he did with a lot of things. *Got a problem? No big deal. Here's some money so I don't have to think about it anymore.* Heaven help any woman who got involved with a man like this.

Not that she was in any danger of that. She was pretty sure she'd made it clear that she wasn't responsive to him. He must have picked up on things she'd said and the way she'd said them. He couldn't be so dense—or so egotistical—that he thought she would be interested.

He was trying to make a call again, then muttered something and swore softly. "So where the hell did they disappear to, anyway?" he said.

She frowned, then realized with a start that he was talking about Jeremy and Fabio. She hadn't given them a thought for some time now. Silently, she scolded herself. Here she'd just been thinking about how dangerous it would be to care about a man like Adam, and the next thing she knew, he gave her raw evidence that she was letting his presence turn her head as it was.

"I'd better go take a look and see if I can find them," he said, rising. "Be right back."

She nodded but didn't speak, glad for a moment to steady herself. But she only had seconds to do that, because her friend Gino arrived just as Adam left.

"Hey, Elena," he said, slumping down into a chair beside her. "Isn't that Adam Ryder?"

Elena's head rose in surprise. "Yes. Do you know him?"

"No. But you seem to." Gino didn't sound pleased. "Is he a friend of yours?"

"I met him yesterday at the ruins."

"Did you?" Gino cleared his throat thoughtfully. "You don't realize who he is, do you?"

She went very still. "No. Tell me."

He patted her hand as though she needed consoling.

"You're not keeping up with the local news, my sweet. He's the latest candidate they've brought in to audition for the job of King of Niroli. He's the illegitimate son of the late crown prince, Antonio."

CHAPTER THREE

ELENA gasped. Adam was Crown Prince Antonio's son? Such a possibility hadn't entered her mind. And he'd seemed like—what? Not an everyday, average guy. Not that. She'd sensed something edgier, more dangerous about him from the first. But hardly royal.

Still, why not? He had the insolence for royalty. No wonder she'd been instinctively wary of him from the beginning. The illegitimate son of Antonio. She could hardly believe it.

"He didn't let on?" Gino asked.

"He gave no hint that I was aware of."

"Hmm. Maybe he thinks he's going incognito for now." Gino grimaced. "Well, be careful, darling. Royalty aren't like you and me. Even when they're illegitimate." He rose. "I've got to see a man about a painting. I'll stop by and see you later."

She nodded. "Don't forget about tonight," she reminded him, thinking of the small gathering of friends she was having that evening.

He bent to kiss her cheek. "I won't let you down," he said affectionately, then hurried off.

His words echoed in her mind and she shook her head to rid herself of them. She seemed, suddenly, to be clinging to any hint of protection as though she was expecting a major assault on her peace of mind very soon. This was no good and it wasn't like her. Ever since she'd been very young she'd worked hard at being self-sufficient. The temptation was to relax and let others take care of her. It came with the territory and she had a very big excuse for doing exactly that. But she knew she would lose all self respect if she let that happen.

Still, this news that Adam was Antonio's son was disturbing. Of all people for her to have run into at the ruins! She almost felt as though she'd stepped into a part of Nirolian history herself while visiting her ancestors.

The island had been in turmoil ever since the fateful day, two years before, when King Giorgio's two sons, his only direct heirs, were killed in a yachting accident, along with one of their wives. Crown Prince Antonio had been particularly beloved by many factions in Niroli. It had been assumed he would soon be King himself, and his death had sent shock waves through every level of society.

The old king's grief had been staggering and he had lost his will to govern. But when he had begun looking around at his grandchildren for a successor, he'd found that one after another they proved unsuitable or unwilling. Rumors had been flying that he was about to turn to an illegitimate child of Antonio's, and now it seemed they were right on the money.

"But that is something I don't want to get involved with," she muttered to herself, and at the same time she heard Adam and the others coming back, and Fabio was suddenly there, rubbing against her leg.

To her consternation, Jeremy seemed to be sobbing.

"What have you done to him now?" she asked Adam fiercely, rising from her chair, all thoughts of his possible connection to royalty out the window.

"I haven't done a thing," he responded shortly. "He fell and scraped his knee before I found them. It's bleeding. I'm going to have to find someone with a first-aid kit around here. Any ideas?"

She hesitated, but quickly realized something would have to be done. The man was one thing. She could be cold and dismissive to the man all day long if she felt like it. But the child was hurt and that was another matter. She couldn't just leave him that way.

"Oh, bother!" she said, giving up on her self-imposed rule to keep Adam out of her house. "Come along, then."

Grasping Fabio's halter, she started off down the street. Behind her, she heard the man and the boy following. She could tell that Adam had swung Jeremy up into his arms and was carrying him. That mollified her somewhat. In fact, she was just a bit chagrined that she'd accused him of hurting his son. She would have to be careful about jumping to false conclusions in the future.

Future, her mind was screaming, trying to get her attention. *What future?* But she ignored it and hurried on.

"Where are we going?" Adam asked.

She held her head high. *If it must be done, t'were best done quickly—and bravely,* she told herself.

"To my house," she said aloud.

"What? You live near here?"

"Just around the corner, actually."

"Oh. Well, that's handy."

They turned the corner and Adam nodded to himself. This was just the sort of neighborhood he could picture her living in—quaint and traditional, yet neat and tidy and very well maintained. A sort of old-fashioned storybook lane. It fit.

What amazed him was how confidently she stepped along the walkway. She did have the dog to lead her, but a dog couldn't do it all and she moved as though she wouldn't allow herself a hint of uncertainty. His lopsided grin appeared almost against his will. If he wasn't careful, he was going to start admiring the woman for more than just her very provocative feminine appeal.

She turned in through a neat picket fence to a small white cottage that could have housed the Seven Dwarves. A brightly painted red door beckoned. Window-boxes spilling over with flowers and a small wishing well completed the picture.

Any moment, he thought, *someone is going to start singing "Someday My Prince Will Come", in the background.*

And that thought almost made him laugh out loud. So he was doing prince jokes now.

But he sobered quickly. Every now and then he began to realize just what he was playing around with here.

Much as he needed the funding to stave off the hostile takeover of his company, was he really willing to trade in his freedom for a crown? He was going to have to decide soon. He was rapidly working his way into a position where he wasn't going to have any choice in the matter.

The inside of the cottage looked as carefully maintained as the outside. The furniture appeared to be antiques lovingly saved from centuries past. And as a centerpiece to the room, a beautiful piano gleamed in the light coming in from the high windows.

He put Jeremy, still sniffling a bit, on the couch while Elena went to a cupboard and found disinfectant and bandages. He watched her, trying to see how she knew where to stand and where to reach. So far he hadn't caught her in a mistake, and that seemed remarkable.

She let him take care of the wound, which seemed to make sense, though he was clumsy at it. Jeremy whimpered a bit when he put on the disinfectant and she went to the piano and began playing him happy tunes to take his mind off it and lift his spirits.

Adam could tell right away that she played beautifully, with the sort of emotion that touched even hardened hearts like his. Jeremy was intrigued, and once he was bandaged up he wanted to go to the piano and sit beside Elena on the bench. She began teaching him a few simple notes and he was eager to try them.

Adam watched for awhile, impressed that she seemed to have a natural way with children—or with his child, at any rate. He'd watched others try to reach Jeremy—

nannies and teachers—and bomb out, totally. In fact, he'd about come to the conclusion the kid was unreachable. But Elena treated him in a normal way and he seemed to like her for it. Maybe there was hope after all.

It wasn't the way she acted, he decided after watching for a few more minutes. It was who she was that got through to the boy. They just had a spontaneous connection. Funny. He wished he knew a way to create that with his son himself.

He didn't usually wallow in the pain of his failed relationships, but for just a moment he let regrets surface. Why was it that he couldn't bond with his boy? Why had Melissa, Jeremy's mother, found it impossible to stay and create a family with them? Why had his own mother spent most of his childhood flitting around the playgrounds of the world instead of being at home, raising him? Was there something in him that pushed all these people away?

He indulged in a short, very obscene oath under his breath to erase that kind of thinking. Life was what it was. You could take it or leave it. But there was no room for whining.

Pushing away from the wall where he'd been leaning, he left the room to go outside and try his cell phone again. It was his only lifeline to his precious company—the one part of his life that had worked out beautifully. He had to save his company from the takeover. After years as a golden boy in the business, he was facing a sort of failure, and suddenly no one was returning his calls. If something didn't happen fast—as in funds becoming available for quick use—it was going to be all over. That was why this delay in settling the crown succession thing was so frustrating. Retaining control of his company meant retaining his sense of identity. The head of Ryder Productions was who he was and what made him special. If he lost that—no, it didn't bear thinking of.

The phone still wasn't working for him and he began to pace about the yard to let off steam. He quickly became curious about Elena's property and what sort of trees she'd planted. The atmosphere was just as pleasant outside as in and, just wandering about, he began to relax. There was a small stone terrace with a table and two chairs under an umbrella and a bank of colorful flowers. A tiny house just steps away from the main building was outfitted with twin beds and a wardrobe. Evidently the building had once served as a garage, then been renovated. He stared at it, wondering who used it. Then he went back into the cottage to find Elena playing tunes from *Peter and the Wolf* and Jeremy dozing with his head in her lap.

He stood in the doorway for a moment, watching the tranquil scene. It seemed like a picture from another era, another place, as though he were looking through time, and maybe through the gauze of memory. A certain yearning crept into his heart as he stood there.

Very deliberately, he pushed it away. What did this have to do with the rat-race world he lived in today? Nothing. It was certainly a seductive destination, but it was an existence built in the clouds. It had no relation-ship to his reality and he knew it would be dangerous to grow too enamored of it.

She came to the end of her piece and he said, "It looks like you've got the magic touch where Jeremy is concerned."

Her dark head lifted. "He seems to be asleep, doesn't he?"

"That he does. Who knew he would respond so well to Prokofiev?" he said.

"Ah, you know your composers," she said, as though that delighted her.

He hated to burst her bubble, but he didn't want to pretend to a sophistication he just didn't have.

"Not really. I know the music to *Peter and the Wolf* because I just produced a series for an educational channel that did a treatment of it. The puppet version."

"Oh."

She actually looked a bit deflated. Why should she care if he knew classical music? It touched him, and at the same time it disturbed him that she felt that way. Was she looking for a connection? Did he want her to?

This woman and her contradictions baffled him. He was used to straightforward dealings with women. Either they attracted him or they didn't. Either he hired them or he didn't. Either he dated them or he didn't. Elena Valerio didn't fit into any of those slots.

"You produce films for television?" she asked as she closed the lid of the piano.

"Yes. Theatrical releases as well. I have a production company in Los Angeles. "

She nodded, her hand falling quietly onto Jeremy's forehead, where she stroked the hair back off his face. Watching her was once again doing strange things to Adam's emotions and he wasn't sure why.

"Here," he said gruffly. "I'll put him on the couch."

He transferred the boy quickly, trying to ignore her spicy scent as he bent close. Luckily, Jeremy didn't stir a bit. Once he had him settled, he turned back to their lovely hostess.

"Your playing is wonderful," he said, and, to his surprise, his genuine feeling was plain in his voice.

"Thank you."

He noticed she didn't bother with false modesty. He liked that. He was used to dealing with artists and other creative types and he understood her quiet confidence in her expertise. It was nice to know she had the artistry to back it up. Walking back into the central area of the room, he leaned against the piano.

"Is that your main talent?"

Something about the question made her turn. "Yes, actually." Her smile was bitter-sweet. "Some would say it's my only talent."

"I don't believe that for a moment." He said the words in all sincerity. He knew she must be good at a lot of other things. She came across as so competent. "Do you ever play professionally?"

She smiled, surprised and gratified by the question. Most people just assumed that because she was blind, she couldn't possibly do anything professionally. She hesitated, toying with the urge to tell him about her acceptance at the New York School of Music Applications. But there wasn't really any point in talking about it. Classes for the current session were only days away and she had no way to get there, much less to pay for living there once she arrived. It was a nice dream, but right now that was all it was.

"I teach music," she said instead, leaving it at that. "That's how I make my living."

He nodded. Looking around the room, he had to conclude the living she made was minimal. Everything was clean and shiny, but a bit worn around the edges at the same time. His gaze drifted back to where she was sitting and he realized he could look at her at will—a sort of feast of the senses—without the usual need to pretend disinterest.

And she was lovely to look at. Today she was dressed in a sort of muted peach shade and the scarf braided in her hair was the color of pomegranates. He wondered briefly how she knew what color she was picking out. That sort of thing was so important to women. He hoped there was someone to help her choose.

This dress was loose and low-cut, displaying the upper swell of her breasts in a way that stirred the senses. He let his gaze slide over her, taking in the curve of her neck and the delicate cut of her collar-bone. Her skin was smooth and seemed to glow in the golden light. He wanted to touch her. And he knew she would kill him if he tried. In a metaphorical way, of course.

And that brought him back to something he'd been wondering about before—just what were her romantic entanglements?

"Do you live here alone?" he asked, glancing around the room and finding nothing particularly masculine in the entire scene.

She nodded.

"No partner? No relationship?"

She smiled. "Why do you ask?"

"I'm just curious. This island seems to have such a great atmosphere for lovers. I'd hate to think you were wasting it."

She threw back her head and laughed out loud. "Oh, you are a devil, aren't you? Actually, having lived here all my life, I'm pretty much immune to the romantic charms of the place."

"So you say." He studied her. "What's your lover like, then?" He could hardly believe she didn't have one.

"My lover? Ah-h-h." She drew in a sensual breath and straightened her spine in a stretch, as though savoring the thought of him, and Adam winced. He didn't need details. Actually, he'd been hoping she was between loves right now.

"My lover has strong arms," she was saying wistfully, "sweet breath, a body like a Greek god. He can sing like an angel, but for nobody but me." She flashed him a quick grin as though waking from a dream. "At least that was the way I imagined him when I was about fourteen."

The sense of relief he felt was ridiculous. "So this isn't a real guy?"

"Oh, I'm sure he's out there somewhere."

He shook his head, enjoying her and not sure if he should be. "You're a strange woman."

She cocked her head to the side. "Different from what you're used to?"

"Infinitely."

"Brilliant. It will probably do you good to shake up your expectations a bit. Maybe you'll get a better picture of what women are really like."

"Play me something," he said softly.

She slowly lifted the piano lid again and her hands went back to the keys, her fingers hitting a few notes softly, but her face was very still. "What would you like to hear?"

"Anything you'd like to play."

She smiled and touched the keys, and in seconds music filled the room. He didn't know what it was, but he knew it was gorgeous—full of fire and passion and a strain of sentimentality that grabbed hold of his heart and soul in a way he wasn't expecting. Emotion grew inside him in response, almost making it hard to breathe. And another thing he hadn't bargained for—watching her playing was arousing him in ways he didn't remember having been aroused before.

But this wasn't just the music—it was mostly the musician.

She hit the final crescendo and her shoulders sagged, as though the music that had filled her was spent. He waited as the sound slowly evaporated into the air of the room.

"Wow," he said, in awe of her power. It was going to

take a moment or two to let his senses stop reeling. "What was that?"

She shrugged, smiled and seemed to regain her strength quickly. "Just some Rachmaninov," she said as though it were everyday stuff.

"You have a thing for the Russians?"

She laughed and it animated her whole body. Watching her, he was filled with a sudden need to take her into his arms and hold her close. This was more than desire, more than sexual hunger. What was it? A protective instinct? He shook his head. Where were these strange feelings coming from?

He reacted to women all the time—he knew what that felt like. But this was different. This included another component and he wasn't sure he wanted to analyze it too closely.

"When it comes to music," she was saying, starting to rise from the piano bench, "I plead guilty as charged."

She moved gracefully and he watched her, much as he might watch a bird in flight, appreciating every move and wanting to see more. He had a hunch she would dance almost as beautifully as she played, if only she could feel secure enough in her surroundings.

She offered him a cool drink and he followed her into the kitchen, watching as she efficiently reached for the glasses, the ice, the bottles of flavored water, without missing a beat. The space was small and compact and she obviously knew where everything was. Still, her confident speed impressed him.

"Do you have everything memorized?" he asked her,

then wondered if she would be offended at his bringing up her blindness.

"Oh, I'm sorry," he began clumsily, then stopped, realizing he was only making things worse.

She turned towards him, shaking her head and half laughing. "Let's get one thing straight right now," she said firmly. "I'm blind, Adam. B-L-I-N-D. Blind! Say it with me. Blind blind blind. I'm not ashamed of it. I'm not denying it. Everybody knows it. You can mention it. It's the elephant in the room and there's no use trying to pretend it isn't there. People who do that tend to trip a lot."

"You're right of course," he said, grinning at how charmingly she was attacking him. "From now on I'll refer to you as that gorgeous blind chick. Okay?"

She put her head to the side. "Hmm. I rather like that."

He wanted to kiss her so badly he could hardly stand it. "Do you know how beautiful you are?" he asked her in all candor. "I mean, do you have any conception of how very attractive you are to…to…" He'd been about to say, "men" but he really meant, "me".

She went motionless for a few seconds, then handed him his drink and turned her face toward his.

"Where's Jeremy's mother?" she asked frankly.

He recognized that question immediately for exactly what it was—a way to remind him that they weren't laying the groundwork for a romance here. She just wasn't interested, and especially not with a man whose current entanglements she didn't have a clear picture of.

But instead of letting it put his back up, he realized

she deserved an honest answer. And, leaning back against the kitchen counter, he decided that was exactly what he would give her.

"The woman who gave birth to my son is currently working her way through the casting couches of Hollywood," he said with a certain bitterness. "We don't refer to her as Jeremy's mother. She's never been a real mother to him. Right now Melissa is probably one big break away from becoming a household name. One big break or one spectacular scandal. Whichever comes first. We don't ever see her. "

Elena was staggered by the tragedy of Jeremy's situation, and by how calmly Adam laid out the facts, as though they were ordinary and needed no special regrets. "Are you married to her?"

"No." He stirred the ice cubes in his glass and they clinked against the sides. "She was afraid a marriage license would tend to get in the way of her career."

"But motherhood didn't tie her down?"

"Not at all. She dumped it right away. Along with me."

"I see."

She had to admit that gave her new insight into this man's character. If he was the sort of father who stepped up and took responsibility for a child whose mother had abandoned him, despite the fact that he obviously wasn't particularly good with children, maybe he wasn't as bad as she'd taken him for at first. Many men would have thrown up their hands and decided the child was surely someone else's problem.

Still, she couldn't let him know she was prepared to

give him any credit. He was definitely a "give the man an inch, he'll take a mile" type, and she wasn't handing out inches right now.

"In other words, you picked the wrong woman to have a serious relationship with," she noted, purposely playing devil's advocate instead of a sympathizer.

He hesitated and took a sip of cool liquid before he answered. "I guess you could pin that on me. But I haven't seen a lot of evidence that there are many women out there you *can* depend on. Every woman in my life has walked out in one way or another."

Elena stiffened as though his words attacked her as well as the women he was referring to. "That's a bit harsh. Are you trying to tell me you don't know any decent women at all?"

His cynicism was raw and candid. "Let's put it this way. We're all human. We all have selfish motives. It just seems to me that women don't admit it up front. They pretend to have higher ideals and then go right ahead and cheat. You can't count on them."

She threw up a hand. "You've been burned and you'll never trust again. Yes, I've heard it before."

"And you'll hear it again. It's based on truth." He frowned and decided turnabout was fair play. "How about you?"

"Me?" She looked surprised at the question.

"Yes, you. You may be proudly blind, but I'm sure you have a love life, too."

"A love life." She laughed out loud at the term. "Sorry to disappoint you. I avoid heartbreak right up front. I don't fall in love. Never have, never will. That makes me almost bulletproof."

"What about your friend, the one who draws nudes?"

"Gino? He doesn't date women."

"Yes, you implied that before."

"You see?" she said again with an impudent smile. "Bulletproof."

She turned and walked off and he watched her go. He didn't believe a word she'd said. She was at least in her mid-twenties and no woman that attractive could have avoided male attention that long.

Did that mean she was just like all the others—making up truth as she went along? He winced. And suddenly he realized he was fighting that concept. He didn't want to think she was like that. In fact, he needed her to be better than that. So what kind of fool was he, anyway?

Draining his glass, he put it down on the counter and followed her back into the living room. She was at the piano lightly playing a soft tune, but she made room for him on the piano bench.

"I took a look at your backyard," he told her. "It's very nice."

She nodded, smiling. "I like to work in the garden, but, of course, I do have some logistical problems. I have a friend who's a landscaper. He comes by and does basic maintenance for me every now and then."

He frowned. Another "he" friend, huh? And she claimed there was no love in her life. But that was really none of his business, was it?

"I noticed a little house out back. Who stays there?"

"Oh, that's the guest house." She lifted her fingers from the keys as she thought about it. "My grandmother had it fixed up for friends who came to stay. When you live in a place like Niroli, you get a lot of visitors."

"So it's ready to go."

"Ready to go?" She looked wary. "What do you mean?"

"I mean it's move-in ready. And I'd like to move in."

"What?" The shock of that concept flashed through her. She could hardly think she'd heard him right.

"Jeremy and I need a place to stay. Your little guest house would be perfect."

"No." She was shaking her head vehemently. With every ounce of emotional strength, she felt herself rejecting the idea. "Oh, no. No, that won't work."

"Sure it will."

Her heart was beating very fast. Her adrenaline was even flowing. Every part of her knew this was not an option. She could not have Adam Ryder living here with her for the duration. It just couldn't be. She rose from the piano bench and backed away from where he still sat. Her hand went to her throat and flattened protectively.

"No," she said with pure passion. "Don't you see? That is absolutely impossible."

CHAPTER FOUR

"IT CAN'T happen," Elena insisted. "You don't belong here. It's impossible."

Adam sat where he was on the piano bench and stared at her. He loved the way her entire body seemed to be consumed with whatever emotion she was feeling. It was almost as though the communications that might have been made by her eyes were instead made by every cell in her body. She was a symphony of the heart, a ballet of the soul. He felt as though he could watch her for ever.

Or at least until things got a little too intense. Watching her body language stirred some body response of his own. Physical communication. He'd never been more ready to try it—at least in theory. Because he knew very well that wasn't going to happen. She was untouchable.

He wasn't usually so attuned to the subtleties of life, especially where women were concerned. He worked in an industry that was rife with beautiful females, and many of them were readily available to an attractive man in his position. There was a temptation in that environment to use women like disposable toys. He'd been guilty of it a time or two himself.

But he'd known right away that Elena could never be a part of something so banal. And it wasn't just because she was blind. There was more, an innocence to her, a purity of spirit that he knew he didn't have the right to sully. She was sacrosanct. And for once in his life, he was going to honor that. Too bad he couldn't think of any straightforward way to let her know that she didn't have anything to worry about on that score.

"You're not giving my idea a fair chance," he told her. "We can make it work." He shrugged, knowing he wasn't being very persuasive but not sure how he could do better. "Think it over for awhile. Go over all the ramifications. Don't let your first impulse rule your head. Take some time and—"

"I don't need time to know that having you here just won't work," she said firmly. "You…you…"

When she couldn't come up with the words, he tried to help. "I what? Bother you in some way?"

Her cheeks reddened so quickly, it was obvious she'd already been thinking along those lines.

"Okay, I promise to try hard not to bother you. In any way. We'll be out there in the little house, quiet as mice. You'll hardly know we're there."

He knew he was blowing smoke and so did she. She didn't even bother arguing his points, turning on him with a new tact instead.

"Are you doing this just because you think the hotel is angry with you over the wedding-cake incident? I'm sure the money you gave them has gone a long way toward clearing that up. If you just go back and—"

"It's not really that," he told her earnestly. "That's only part of it. There's a lot more." He hesitated. It was probably time to come clean. Maybe past time. "I... well, I really haven't told you everything..."

"About how you're supposed to be interviewing to become the next King of Niroli?" she interjected quickly, thinking he would never get to the crux of the matter if she waited for his halting explanation. And she needed this cleared up right away. He couldn't stay here!

"So what? If you don't like the hotel, why don't you just go stay at the palace? I would have thought that would be where you would want to be anyway."

"Not hardly," he said, studying her with surprise. How had she figured out that he was in line for the crown? The news must be more widely known than he'd realized. And that was not good. It only emphasized how important it was for him to hide out someplace like this.

"How did you know?" he asked her curiously.

"Gino told me."

"Ah, the ubiquitous Gino." He was rapidly developing a firm dislike for the man. "He gets around a lot, doesn't he?"

"Gino is one of my best friends," she insisted sharply. "He knows more about what's going on around town than most people do."

"Good for him," he replied dryly. "Then I'd appreciate it if you didn't pass this on to him, but, as far as the palace goes, I'm in the bargaining phase right now. I don't want to stay there because I need distance and a way to make them wonder if I'm really interested. You understand negotiation, don't you?"

"You mean manipulation, don't you?" she shot back, beginning to pace on the Persian carpet.

He grinned. "Okay. I'll accept that word. But you can see why I don't want to stay where the palace bureaucrats can keep tabs on me twenty-four hours a day."

"Then try another hotel."

"I don't want a hotel. The press has already been nosing around. All I need is for the local paparazzi to start peeking in my window. I have to stay someplace where nobody knows my name."

She stopped before him, almost pleading. "Adam, it's a small island. You can't hide here like you can in a big city."

"I can lay low for a little while. Put off the inevitable. I'll pay you well for the place."

"Oh!" She went back to pacing. She didn't want him here. She couldn't have him here. She'd never wanted him in her house in the first place. And now he wanted to stay!

No. It was impossible. He was too big, too loud, too overwhelming. It had been bad enough having him hanging around all afternoon. She'd been on edge, unable to really relax. She couldn't be like that for days at a time. This was her space. She didn't want him in it.

The front door banged and Adam spun in surprise. A tall man with a hard, wiry build was coming into the house. Handsome in a self-conscious way, he looked tough and a bit petulant.

"Hello," he said to Elena. "I just dropped by to let you know Devon and Martha can come tonight after all."

"Oh, good," she said distractedly, then waved a hand in Adam's general direction. "Gino, meet Adam Ryder."

Adam rose from the piano bench, ready to shake hands, but Elena's friend didn't seem to be in a hand-shaking mood.

"Oh." Gino looked at Adam but he didn't look pleased. "What's he doing here?"

Elena threw up her hands. "I don't know. Why don't you ask him?"

Adam had no problem providing an answer. "Right now I'm trying to get Elena to rent out her little guest house to me."

Gino's brows drew together menacingly. "Well, she's not going to do that."

Adam raised an eyebrow as a counter-measure. "Isn't she?" he said quietly.

"No. Of course not. She can't have you here."

Elena turned, listening intently, her lips pressed tightly together.

"She won't do it," Gino went on confidently. "She doesn't need you. Look, we know who you are."

"Do you?"

"You're Adam Ryder. You've got ties to the royal family."

"You got me there. Not that it's anything to brag about."

"What? Our royal family isn't good enough for you?"

The man was obviously ready to take anything he said as an affront. Adam smiled. "It's a complicated situation," he said calmly.

"Well, Elena doesn't need that sort of complication in her life."

Gino was glaring in a way that said he was used to being able to intimidate, but Adam held his gaze with a cool response in his own.

"I have no intention of complicating Elena's life."

"But you didn't tell her who you were right away, did you? You were trying to keep it a secret. You're not an honest man."

Elena's head rose at that and she stepped between them. "Gino, that's enough. This is my decision, not yours."

Gino's anger made him reckless. "Elena, sometimes you just have to admit you could use some help."

"Gino!"

He grabbed her hands and gazed down at her earnestly. "Look, I know you just lost half your income and you're frantic to figure out how to replace it. Especially as you are trying to find a way to pay for attending that music program in New York."

"That's right," she said tartly. "So you should understand."

"But, darling, this is not the way to do it," he said, pleading with her and at the same time making it clear that he expected her to do exactly what he suggested. "We'll find a better way. I'll sell a painting. Just give it some time."

Adam waited quietly through this exchange. He'd seen her face while Gino was spouting off orders and he allowed himself a small smile. She didn't like being told what to do, and she really didn't like being told she needed someone to take care of her. There was still a chance here. All he had to do was wait Gino out and then play his cards right. He was a negotiation pro from way back. He knew how to do this.

"Elena, listen to reason. You can't do it." Gino looked as though he were about to stamp his foot.

But Elena was having none of it. She held her chin high and looked rebellious. "I'll make that decision on my own."

Gino gave an exasperated sigh and turned toward the door. "I've got no more time for chit-chat," he said, sounding more than annoyed. "I'm due at the spa. I promised Natalia I'd give her some help decorating. She's completely redoing some of the exercise rooms." He glared back at Adam, his look purposefully ominous. "I'll have to deal with all this later, including you," he said in menacing tones.

And he was out the door.

Adam turned to grin at Elena. He knew she couldn't see it, but she would surely hear it in his voice.

"When he says "deal with all this later", what exactly is he talking about?" he asked her, tongue in cheek.

"Oh, pay him no mind," she said in exasperation. "Gino has a flair for the dramatic. He's mostly talk."

"'Mostly', huh? It's that little margin of doubt that tends to give one pause. The unknown factor is always the deadly one. So, just the same, I guess I'll keep my guard up."

He wasn't really rattled by Gino's implied threat. He'd faced down bigger men than Elena's friend. Still, it didn't hurt to add a little fuel to her resentment for being treated like someone who needed managing.

And he'd certainly taken in all that talk about how desperately she needed funds right now. He knew the feeling—though his financial needs were in a different league. Still, he had plenty of spare cash for the small needs of life.

It was on the tip of his tongue to promise her all the things he could do for her as King, but he stopped himself just in time. He had to be smart about this. The more he analyzed things, the more he realized she would hate something like that. He might as well just lay low. If he played his cards right, she would succumb in the end.

"How much?"

She stopped her pacing and inclined her head, looking like a swan considering possibilities. "How much what?"

"How much do you want to rent the room out? Here's what I was thinking." He named a price that made her gasp. "That's twice what I'm paying at the Ritz."

"For my crummy little room?" she cried.

He shrugged. "Well, you'll also have to let me have the run of your house. After all, there's no bathroom out there. And most of all…" he managed to add a note of tragic regret "…most of all, no kitchen."

She shook her head and threw out her hands. A half-smile was playing at the corners of her mouth. "You long for a kitchen of your own, do you?" she murmured.

He smiled and nodded. "It's handy for late night snacks."

She repeated the sum in her head in wonder. Why, if he stayed long enough, she could pay her airfare to New York. Her shoulders sagged and a deep sigh went through her body. There had been a time when she'd considered herself a hard-headed realist. Now she was becoming a greedy little dreamer instead. Was she going to hate herself in the morning?

"You're just like the serpent in the garden, aren't you?"

His head went back. He wasn't sure he liked her choice of analogy. "What are you talking about?"

"Temptation. You're holding out a big fat juicy red apple my way."

He supposed she was right. Still, it seemed an odd way of putting it…for her. "What do you care what color it is?" he asked softly.

"Oh, there's a difference. Believe me. I can feel it." She nodded. "It's big and it's red and it's delicious. Will I break down and take a bite? That's the question."

There was something so sexy about the way she said that. He was glad—and not for the first time—that she couldn't see what the images she conjured up did to him.

"Of course, the money is tempting."

He shrugged. "Sure. Money makes the world go round."

That put her back up quickly enough. "Well, money doesn't make *me* go round. At least not usually."

"Different motivations for different people. What about compassion? How about friendship?"

She gave him a scathing look. "You're not my friend. I barely know you."

"To know me is to love me, so don't worry about that."

She frowned and he regretted his flip attitude. She deserved better.

"You make the rules, Elena," he said quickly. "Whatever you say goes. I promise you that."

She nodded slowly. "I'm considering it," she admitted. "But I do have one condition," she added.

He stood poised, waiting. "What's that?"

She took a deep breath, then said in a calm, steady voice, "I have to see you first."

He went very still. Something was prickling the hairs on the back of his neck. "What are you talking about?"

"I have to 'see' you. Until I really see you, I won't know you well enough to know if I can let you stay here or not." Coming toward him, she pointed toward where a straight-backed chair stood. "Sit down."

"What for?" He resisted, strangely apprehensive.

"Sit down and I'll show you."

He really didn't want to do this. "Are you going to do that touching my face thing? Because I don't really think that's going to tell you anything. I mean—"

"Sit down."

He glanced at his watch, then looked over at the couch where his son was sleeping soundly. "Listen, I've got to be at the palace in a little over an hour for a meeting and—"

"This won't take long. Sit down."

He hesitated, looking at her. She meant it. He wasn't going to talk his way out of this. He sat down.

She came toward him with a purposeful air and suddenly his mouth went very dry. He hadn't been this scared since…since the night Melissa went into labor with Jeremy. But he didn't want to think about that.

He stared straight ahead and she stood next to him for a moment. He had the impression she was taking in the sense of him, and maybe his smell, but that was just a feeling. He couldn't pin it down to any solid clues. And he felt like a fool with his heart beating a mile a minute. At this rate he was going to start to sweat and then he would really feel oafish when she touched him.

She was going to touch him. He was sure of that. And the wait was beginning to drive him over the edge. *Come on,* he wanted to yell. *Touch me! Get it over with.* She was standing so still…

And then her fingers were lightly touching his hair, just barely tracing the outline of his head, so softly it could have been butterfly wings. It was as though she were probing his aura rather than needing a solid tactile experience. He closed his eyes and his pulse slowed. This wasn't so bad. He could stand this. In fact, it felt pretty good. Even when her fingers stiffened and began to rake back into the thickness of his hair, it wasn't so bad. He'd had massages that had felt a lot like this. So far, so good.

And then she shifted her position, as though she wanted to get a better angle on her approach to him. He felt her move and he opened his eyes to find her sliding in between his knees and reaching out with both hands to take hold of his head.

And suddenly he was drowning in sensation. Her hands were moving lightly over his face, touching his eyebrows, running along the ridges of his eye sockets, flattening across the planes of his cheeks. And at the same time her full, peaked breasts, barely covered by low-cut, gauzy cloth, were inches from his face and the outer muscles of her legs were pressing against the incredibly sensitive flesh of his inner thighs. Desire shot through him like a lightning bolt and he was hard as a rock in seconds—and terrified that she would feel it.

He hadn't felt so out of control since he was a teenager and he couldn't let her know. He tried holding his breath, thinking about nursery rhymes, singing old songs in his head. Nothing worked. He was afraid she would notice and be disgusted with him. He didn't want her to think he was all untamed male aggression. She was so clean and genuine. She deserved to be treated with respect.

"I'm almost done," she whispered to him. "Just a moment more."

Her small hands curled around his ears, then slid down to cup his jaw bone. He made a strangled sound, but she didn't seem to notice. She leaned closer in order to touch the back of his head. One tiny move and he could have taken her right nipple into his mouth. The cloth that barely covered her seemed like gossamer now, cobwebs, almost invisible. He could see the nipple, see it tighten. All he had to do was reach out with his tongue…

Oh, God! He was about to explode. He was so hard, he was in pain and it took all his strength not to writhe with it.

Her finger touched his lips, tracing them softly, and he thought, *Just let me die now.* And then it was over.

"There," she said, drawing back in a matter-of-fact way. "All done. Now was that so bad?"

He cleared his throat to cover the fact that he couldn't speak just yet. "Uh…no, not at all," he managed to croak out at last. Looking at her, he shook his head. How could one slender blind woman pack such a wallop? He didn't think he would ever be the same again.

She dropped down to sit on the piano bench, facing where he still sat. He didn't move. He didn't dare to.

"You're a very handsome man, aren't you?" she said calmly.

He swallowed hard and tried to focus. "What makes you say that?"

"The evenness of your features." She smiled. "And your cocky attitude. But that doesn't matter, because I can't see you the way other people do. What does matter is how beautiful your character is. Tell me about that, Adam. What kind of shape is your character in? What kind of a person are you?"

Her words might have been just the cold shower he needed. Talk about turning a pleasure into something painful. Contemplating his character was not something he did very often. Probably because he wasn't sure he was going to like what he found there.

"My character has its ups and downs," he said evasively. "But I can promise you this. I won't do anything to hurt you while I'm here. I swear it."

She sat quietly, mulling that over. She knew which way she was leaning but she forced herself to slow down and think it through. This man was planning to become King. That put him way out of her circle. He was one of the most cynical men she'd ever known. That should have put him even further out of her range. And finally, she found herself dangerously drawn to him—an attraction that had no future. All the elements for disaster were there. So that meant she was going to turn him down, didn't it? Make him leave—never see him again. Save herself and her "bulletproof" love life. It was only logical.

But this was the new Elena she was dealing with, the woman who'd awakened from her sleepwalk and wanted to engage with the world. He needed a place to stay. She could certainly use the money. It was only logical.

He finally confronted her with the question of the hour.

"Well? Do I pass muster? Are you going to rent me a room?"

Slowly, she nodded. "Yes," she said almost regretfully. "Yes, Adam. I'm going to rent you a room. At least for a little while."

Moving in didn't take any time at all. Once the bargain had been made, Adam used Elena's telephone to make a few calls and soon his things were brought over from the hotel. He transferred Jeremy from the couch to the second twin bed in the little house. And before she knew it he was off for the palace, and she sat down to catch her breath and mull over what she'd done—and whether she was likely to survive this experience as the same person she'd been up to now.

There were so many reasons why she shouldn't have done it. When she actually let herself dwell on the possible results that could apply, her heart nearly stopped. Here she was, playing with fire again. The last thing in the world she needed was a man hanging around, making her crazy. What was wrong with her? Just that morning she'd tried to avoid speaking to him. Now she was preparing to practically live with him! She had to be crazy.

She knew Gino would be furious. "You're not like a regular person," he would fume. "You can't risk things like this with a stranger."

Gino was one of her very best friends and had been for years. In the past she'd always thought his watchfulness a bit touching. Now she began to realize it was becoming patronizing and overbearing. As sure as could be, he would make plans to sleep on her couch to protect her. She'd better think fast to be prepared with reasons why that would be impossible. She didn't want him there— and she wasn't going to think about why that might be.

Still, she knew he was probably right. She did need protection—from herself.

That thought made her laugh, and she knew it wasn't really true. No, she wasn't yet that crazy. But she had to admit she was intrigued with Adam.

When she'd told Adam she'd never been in love, she'd been telling the honest truth. Growing up, she'd had the same hopes and dreams as all girls had, but that had always been tempered by the knowledge that she couldn't expect to have the same sort of life her friends had. She was different.

Her mother and grandmother, when they were alive, had both agreed that she was different, but they'd emphasized the fact that she was special, not strange. She'd always known she had an exceptional talent for music. It came naturally. Her grandmother had been a soloist in the Nirolian National Choir when she was young and her mother had worked as a music archivist for years. She'd always known, one way or another, music would be her life.

And that had given her the strength to shy away from romance all these years. When her grandmother urged her to date one of the many young men who pursued her, she would laugh and shake her head. "The man for me will be unique," she would say. "I'll know him when I hear his voice."

Was she dreaming or merely making excuses to fend off the advice? As she looked back now that young woman seemed utterly naïve. What did she think—her ideal man would walk into her life and she would know it by the sound of his voice? That was indeed dreaming.

She hadn't liked the sound of Adam's voice at first. She'd thought he sounded conceited and arrogant, and she'd hated the way he talked to his son. Now that she knew him better, she'd modified her judgement. But he still was nowhere near being that wonder man she'd thought she was waiting for.

Still, she had to admit he was stirring feelings in her she hadn't known she had. When she'd touched his face, she'd felt a sense of wonder she'd never felt before. She wanted to touch him again.

And she wanted him to touch her. And that was where the danger lay. Just thinking about it made her gasp. She was going to have to be very careful.

Especially since, much as he appealed to her on a personal level, she was having doubts about his mission here. She was beginning to wonder if she could really get behind the effort to make him King. She loved her island home and she wanted a good king. And preferably one who loved Niroli, too. She was noticing more and more evidence that Adam might not be that person.

His attitude was very disturbing. At first, she'd noticed him take a crack at her homeland here and there, but she'd attributed that to his generally cynical outlook. It wasn't until he'd been just about to leave for the palace that she'd found him saying things that had really set her back on her heels. Had he really meant them? And could she overlook his attitude?

CHAPTER FIVE

ELENA and Adam had been in the little house and he'd been searching through his luggage for a tie.

"Seems an odd thing to wear on Niroli," she said with a laugh.

"I know. Most disappointing." He must have found one because she heard him place himself in front of the mirror and begin working with something. "But I was warned it would be wise to wear one, and, until I have the crown in my hot little hands, I figure I'll be better off taking their hints seriously."

"That would seem wise," she murmured.

"I'm hoping to get to meet the old man tonight," he added.

"The old man?" His tone horrified her and she turned slowly toward him. "Are you talking about the king? Your grandfather?"

"That's the one."

She frowned, genuinely disturbed by this way of speaking about her monarch. "Don't you think you should have a little more respect?"

"For whom?" he shot back bitterly. "For the man who banished my mother from the kingdom so that he would never have to acknowledge me? The man who now finds he needs me after all, so is ready to throw blossoms at my feet? That's the man I'm supposed to respect?"

"Yes. If you can't respect the man himself, at least respect his position. He's our King!"

"Not for much longer," he muttered. "Then I guess you'll be telling people to respect *me*, won't you?"

"Of course."

He laughed and chucked her under the chin. "You're cute as a button, Elena, but you're wrong."

And that was where things had stood as he'd left for the palace.

Once he'd gone, Elena had stewed over what he'd told her for awhile, and then she'd called Susan Nablus, an old friend of her mother's and an expert on Nirolian history. If anyone could give her the straight scoop on what had happened around the time of Adam's conception, she could. Susan had just come in from shopping, but she was delighted to hear from Elena and she promptly sat down and offered to answer any questions her old friend's daughter might have.

"Adam Ryder, you say. So that's his name. Well, I had heard rumors that the powers that be at the palace were considering him, since they've run through all the more direct contenders and come up empty."

"As Antonio's son, I'd say he's pretty directly related," Elena protested.

"Yes, dear, but he's illegitimate. And his mother has no standing."

"I guess that is the point," Elena conceded.

"I never met Adam, but I did meet his mother when she was here. My, it was over thirty years ago, wasn't it? I believe her name was Stephanie. She was quite beautiful, one of those socialites with the good cheekbones who become supermodels for a few years, appear on the covers of all the magazines, then fade from sight—like those beautiful confections that melt away in the heat of the sun. My impression was that she was just one of those sweet, pretty girls who get passed around by playboys. She came to Niroli for a fashion shoot. It was just a couple of years after that horrible kidnapping where one of the prince's twins was snatched. They said Antonio had been a perfect husband before that happened. Well, losing one of your babies is enough to unhinge anyone, I suppose.

"At any rate, Prince Antonio caught a glimpse of Stephanie and a moment later he was over the moon. Poor Princess Francesca had to endure a lot from her wayward husband after the kidnapping, but I think that affair was the worst for her. It was so public, you know. As far as the media was concerned, it was an affair to remember and the little wife and remaining baby sitting at home were old news."

"Poor thing," Elena commented.

"Yes. Well, it didn't last long. Suddenly Stephanie was gone and the prince seemed bereft, but he managed to go back to his duties and soon it was almost as though it had never happened. He and Francesca had two more children and seemed quite devoted as the years went by. It was only later that we found out that Stephanie had been hustled out of the country once the king found out about her, and that she was pregnant at the time."

"So she *was* banished by King Giorgio."

"Oh, yes. Never to set foot on these shores again, et cetera et cetera. Of course, I'm sure they gave her plenty of money to keep her quiet."

"Money." Elena nodded. That did seem to be a common theme with the Ryder family. And that thought gave her a dull, unpleasant feeling in the pit of her stomach.

But that feeling faded as she spent the rest of the afternoon preparing for her evening party. Jeremy woke up and was completely agreeable, playing with Fabio, then helping her with the canapés and negotiating more piano lessons in a clever way that made her think he had more of his father in him than Adam realized.

She didn't know if Adam would be back in time to join her entertainment. From what he'd said, she was pretty sure he would be engaged at the palace until fairly late that night. And he hadn't exactly brimmed with enthusiasm for her party.

"I'm having some people over tonight," she told him as he was preparing to leave for his meeting. "So when you get back…"

"Don't worry. I'll keep out of your way."

That wasn't what she'd been about to say. In fact, she'd been about to invite him to join them.

"Actually, I'd rather as few people as possible know about me being here," he reminded her.

"I understand," she said, though she was disappointed.

"How many people do you suppose already know?" he asked her.

"Well, there's Gino, of course."

Adam laughed shortly. "Can we have him bound and gagged and held in a cellar for a few days?"

She smiled but said, "No."

"Damn." He turned toward her. "Still, if no one but Gino knows I've been here, we might be alright. I was hoping I would have a day or two before the hyenas descend."

"I've never known a man so sure he was at the center of the universe," she said, only half teasing.

And yet, he had reason to feel as though everyone had him in their sights. Right now, he was the man of the hour in Niroli. How odd to think that she had that very man right here with her. It *was* rather exciting.

The hour was late when Adam got back. He took a cab from the palace and had it drop him off in downtown Monte Speziare, then walked the few blocks to Elena's house. He could see that she still had people with her. The sound of talk and laughter followed him as he went to check on Jeremy, who was sound asleep once again in the guest house, probably exhausted from meeting all of Elena's friends and romping with the dog. He paused for a brief space of time, looking at the boy. He looked so angelic in sleep. And for just a moment, Adam felt love swell in his heart.

If only he knew how to reach out to Jeremy, to make him into a real son instead of an annoying charge and an antagonist. If only he knew how Elena did it. If only a lot of things.

Going out into the yard, he made another attempt to get through to his business partner in Los Angeles and finally made the connection. Zeb had only bad news to report. Celluloid Images, the firm trying to buy out Ryder Productions, had petitioned to file final papers. If he didn't get some funds soon, he would lose his company. He had to close this deal.

He completed the call and tried to push aside the feeling of doom it had brought on. His meeting at the palace hadn't given him much to hope for, either. In fact, the more he met with these people, the more he wondered if he could bring off this royal makeover in a convincing way. The counselors had tried to paint a cheery picture of what life as a king would be like, but he could see through their fantasies. He was going to be working hard for the money. And how he was going to get out of some of the strictures, such as having to stay here in Niroli full time, he wasn't sure. Still, he would deal with that later. Right now, he just needed the money.

The sounds of the party drew him closer, but he lingered in the backyard garden, reluctant to go in and have to try to explain to Elena's friends who he was and why he was living there. She must have told them something to explain Jeremy. He didn't want to complicate matters.

But he wanted to see her. And suddenly, there she

was through the window. She looked like an angel. His heart started to pound just looking at her. She'd finally shed her dark glasses and her eyes were huge, dark and luminous. She'd freed her hair and it fell in wispy ringlets all around her shoulders. She wore a strapless sundress, which was spectacularly form-fitting, emphasizing the thrust of her breasts and her tiny waist and exposing a lot of smooth, creamy skin. He wanted her so badly, he was beginning to ache for her again—and that was ludicrous! He had to stop this.

But he couldn't stop watching her. She moved with such grace and looked so beautiful.

And more than that, she was so brave. Her vulnerability was deep and abiding and it couldn't be erased from the experiences of her life. And yet, she put herself out there every day, let it all hang out and laid it all on the line. Why couldn't he do that, if only a little bit? He knew it would make him a better person. It slowly began to dawn on him that he admired her as much as he desired her. Maybe more. And all he could do was watch.

Elena's good friend Natalia Carini was helping her clear away the mess from her party. Most of the guests had gone home, but some of her closest friends stayed behind to make sure she didn't get stuck having to do all the clean-up herself.

They'd been laughing over a joke Natalia had made when suddenly her smile faded and she stared out through the window into the dark night.

"Elena, there's a man skulking in your garden," she said.

Elena's head came up. "What sort of man?" she asked, a thread of interest apparent in her voice no matter how she tried to disguise it.

"Tall. Handsome." Natalia laughed softly. "He just winked at me."

"Ah." A feeling of excitement swept through her, though she tried her best to suppress it. "That must be Jeremy's father."

"I see." Natalia leaned over the counter to get a better look at him. "He seems lonely out there, don't you think?"

Elena nodded, fighting back a smile. "I'll go out and see if he needs anything."

Natalia turned and pretended to scold. "I'm not sure I approve of you dallying with strange men in the garden."

"He *is* strange," Elena admitted with a laugh, "but I can handle him."

Lisa and Ted Barone had lived in the neighboring house for years, so knew Elena about as well as anyone. It was Lisa who, witnessing this, turned and called softly to her husband. "Will wonders never cease? Elena has a man in her life."

Elena had started for the door, Fabio trotting right beside her, but she turned back at that. "No, I don't," she said uneasily. "No, no! This is not a man in my life."

Lisa struck a pose. "Really? What is it, then? A giraffe? A leopard?"

Natalia shook her head as though she was sorry, but had to side with Lisa. "Looks like a man to me."

Elena had to laugh. Her friends were being annoying, but in a good way. "He's a man all right. But he's not in my life. Not in the intimate way you mean."

"Bring him in," Natalia urged, "and let us make the judgment call."

And so she did. She went out into the cool night air and zeroed in on where he was standing right away.

"Adam?"

"Right here."

He leaned down to pet Fabio, then agreed to come in and meet her friends. Still, to cover the bases, they went over a quick game plan first.

"I know you don't want to use your real name," she said, thinking. "It has been in the papers. So-o-o…let's see. We'll call you Rex."

"Rex?" He grimaced, not at all sure about that. "Don't they call dogs Rex?"

"And kings," she reminded him. "But you need a last name, too. And it should be relevant so we can always claim there was a point to this. How about Hollywood?"

"Rex Hollywood?" He groaned. "I may be something of a sham, Elena, but I'm not that kind of a phony. Anyway, technically, my base production center is in Burbank, not Hollywood."

"Rex Burbank? Perfect." She beamed, pleased with the results of their attempt at skullduggery.

And so Rex Burbank was who he became to her friends. He met them one by one and was charming and personable to each. The only one who had a problem with him was the predicable one— Gino.

"Rex Burbank?" he said in unalloyed disgust. But he shook hands and didn't say any more once Elena had jabbed him in the ribs with her elbow.

"So, *Rex,*" he said when the introductions were over, exaggerating the name to the point where it was almost comical. "How do you like our little island nation?"

Adam shrugged, accepting a drink from Natalia and smiling his thanks. "An island is an island. I've been to lots of them."

A ripple of quiet outrage went through the small crowd around him, but Gino was the one who continued to question him. "You find nothing unique about Niroli?"

Adam looked about at the faces turned up to his and realized he ought to temper his cynicism a bit, for public consumption at least. "Actually I haven't had time to do much looking around," he assured them all. "Once I do, I'm sure I'll start appreciating Niroli's many special qualities."

"Maybe you should do more sightseeing and stop bothering people in their homes instead," Gino said, his chest thrust out confrontationally.

Things might have escalated out of control from there, if Natalia hadn't pulled Adam away to show him a display of early Nirolian musical instruments Elena's mother had collected and kept in a glass case at one end of the living room. There were items that looked very much like violins, others like wind instruments and a set of strangely formed drums. Each had roots in forms that were familiar, but each also had something very unique in its design and development, something contributed by Nirolian natives from centuries past.

"Elena's mother was a music archivist," Natalia explained. "She did a lot of work for the Nirolian National Music Society at the palace twenty years ago or so."

Adam nodded, impressed by the professional look to the display. "I take it she is deceased."

"Yes, she had a heart attack about ten years ago. Luckily, Elena's grandmother was still alive at the time and so she wasn't alone."

"And now she's lost her grandmother, too."

"Yes, fairly recently. But she's strong." Natalia smiled impishly. "You've noticed that, I imagine."

He grinned back at her. "Yes. And I know she wants to be independent."

"Oh, yes. What she wants most right now is to find a way to take advantage of the scholarship she won to that New York music school."

Adam remembered that Gino had hinted about some sort of opportunity overseas. "She won a scholarship?"

"Yes. It's in a program that uses music as a type of therapy for troubled children. The only problem is getting to New York and then paying for housing while she's there. And being able to do it on her own. All that is quite an undertaking for a woman who's been raised in such a small, protective environment. Not to mention a woman who is blind."

"She can do it." He made the claim without the slightest sense of irony. The conviction that she could do just about anything she put her mind to seemed to have implanted itself deep inside him and he had no doubts.

"We all know that," Natalia responded. "But it will be quite difficult. And possibly very painful."

The others caught up with them and the conversation moved in other directions, but Adam couldn't get Natalie's last words out of his head, and he kept looking at Elena, wishing he knew how to make things easier for her in some way. "Difficult....painful." Those shouldn't be factors looming large in the future of a woman like this. And yet, instinctively he knew that trying to protect her from them would be a form of abuse in itself. There were going to be hazards she would have to face on her own. Luckily, she seemed a lot more ready for them than he was to let her experience them. He was going to have to force himself to back off and leave her alone.

But what was he thinking? He wasn't going to be around long enough to be involved in any of that, was he? Even if he became King, Elena wasn't likely to fall into his circle at the palace. Because, if the truth be known, despite all the rules they were throwing at him about how much time he had to spend here, he wasn't planning to make Niroli his permanent home.

"Take the money and run," was pretty much his game plan. All that was left was to see if he could get his plan to execute.

Still, he had a hard time ignoring how appealing Elena was tonight. Her body was enticing and her face was as beautiful as any woman he'd ever seen. And now he had time to study those eyes that she was finally revealing, and he was amazed at how gorgeous they were. They didn't look like most eyes. It was quite evident that no sight was taking place—at least not in the obvious sense. But there was a warmth there, a sort of incandescent perception that was beyond normal vision.

She can't see my face, he thought to himself, *but she can see inside my soul.*

That was, of course, much too fanciful for a man like him to tolerate so he immediately made fun of himself for even thinking it. Still, the concept lingered in his mind and wouldn't let him go. This woman whom he'd only known for hours was looming so large in his view of life, it almost seemed like magic.

Or as if someone had cast a spell on him.

The last holdouts at the party were beginning to contemplate taking their leave. Adam was looking forward to having Elena to himself soon. And he especially anticipated losing Gino's unwelcome company.

The man had dogged him for the entire evening. It was only later that he found out that Elena had told him in no uncertain terms that he was not to sleep on her couch, no doubt adding fuel to his resentment.

Adam had amused himself a few times making slightly disparaging remarks about Niroli just to see Gino rise to the bait like an angry shark. Elena had stepped between them twice before the evening was over, and Gino was obviously boiling.

"I'll be back first thing in the morning and I expect a full report," he said fiercely as he prepared to leave.

"A report of what?" Natalia whispered at Elena's ear.

"Never mind," Elena whispered back.

Natalia laughed. "Poor Gino. He's afraid of losing his little protégé."

But he did leave, and so did the others, calling out their last good wishes as they went. Adam turned to Elena. Her cheeks were pink and her lips were rosy and he wanted to kiss her right there with her friends still in sight. But he didn't.

"I liked your party," he said instead. "It was very urbane, very sophisticated. Very continental."

She smiled, obviously aware he was half teasing, so he went on.

"For living in such a small town, you all seem so…big-city European."

"European?" She laughed. "How would you know what 'European' was like?"

"I've traveled in Europe. Many times."

"Really?" She laughed again. Everything he said was amusing her. "And how did our little gathering compare to your Hollywood parties?"

He turned away in disgust. "Oh, please. Hollywood is full of phonies. I hate Hollywood parties."

He picked up a couple of stray dishes and began to carry them into the kitchen. "There are real people living in Los Angeles, you know. If you've got to go to parties, go to real people parties. Like this one."

"I'll keep that in mind," she said, following him with a pair of wineglasses she'd found.

He turned and looked at her, leaning against the

kitchen counter, while she rinsed out the last few things. "Gino seemed to resent the air space I take up just by breathing," he noted. "I thought you implied he was gay."

"He is."

"Then why does he always look like he wants to fight me to the death over your naked body?"

She turned toward him, her mouth open in mock outrage. "Explain to me why my body would be naked in this fantasy scenario of yours."

He shrugged. Wasn't it self-evident? "You'd be the trophy, of course. The prize." He grinned, contemplating the scene and liking it. "Prizes are always better naked."

She pouted. "Couldn't I have just a little scrap of clothing?"

He shook his head sternly. "No. Not allowed. This is my fantasy. I make the rules."

"I see." She turned back to the washing up with a slight smile. "Remind me to keep my distance from your fantasies in the future."

"Too late." Reaching out, he touched her hair and she went very still. As he continued his voice became very low and husky. "You're becoming the star attraction in my dreams, you know."

Her breath caught jaggedly in her throat and she pulled away from his touch. "To get back to Gino," she said quickly, drying her hands on a towel and starting out of the room, "he and I are very close. We have been for years. So be nice to him, please."

"Be nice to Gino?" he muttered skeptically, but not loud enough for her to hear. He followed her out into the living room. *Speaking of people it's not easy to be nice to,* he added to himself, and aloud he said, "Thanks for taking care of Jeremy while I was gone. How did your evening with him go? Was he civilized?"

"Civilized?" She turned to face him, standing at the piano. "He was a perfect angel. He helped me get ready for the party and then…" She smiled, remembering. "Then he negotiated his way into getting me to give him another piano lesson."

"Really? He's sitting still for lessons?" That surprised him.

She nodded. "He loves them. He asked me to teach him." She let her fingers trail over the piano keys. "He's learning very quickly. A natural." Her smile was impish. "He has something he wants to show you tomorrow. Don't let me forget."

Adam frowned. This did not sound like any son he knew. "Was that his idea or yours?" he asked cynically.

Her head came up and she looked disapproving. "Why do you ask that?"

The impulse to defend himself overcame his good sense. "Because I've never seen any sign that my son gives a damn about me, that's why." It was the first time that he'd ever put the feeling into words. The pain and resentment hung in the air as the sound of his statement evaporated. Her face was registering the shock of it and he wished he'd kept his feelings to himself.

"You're his father," she said at last. "He loves you."

He grimaced and looked around to see if there was a bottle of something strong left out he could take some solace in. "I've known that kid for a long time, Elena," he said quietly. "Where's the evidence?"

She stood where she was, very still. "I think you're looking for it in the wrong places."

He twitched. "And I think you're dreaming." He grabbed a mint out of a bowl set out for the guests and popped it in his mouth. A mint wasn't exactly a good stiff drink, but it would have to do until one came along.

Meanwhile, he wanted to get off of this subject. "Anyway, my evening at the palace was mostly a waste of time. They wanted me to stay for dinner, meet some people. But I'm not sure it was worth the effort. I got the distinct impression that all the important people are still out of town. They just wanted to feel me out a bit."

She frowned, her head bent as she listened to him. She wished she could hear some small sense of an understanding of the history and majesty and wonder of this island and this job he was taking on in his voice. Was it really just a vehicle for money in his eyes? Did he really not care at all?

"Too bad," she said. "And you didn't get to meet with your grandfather?"

"No. He's got a cold or something. I'm pretty sure they are making excuses to keep me from him, but that's hardly important. The contract is the crux of the matter and they haven't let me see it yet."

"Ah." There it was. The money. That was his whole focus.

"Yes, they seem to be balking. Tomorrow I figure I'll take Jeremy in and really give them a run for their money." He popped another mint. "They don't know much about Jeremy yet. Right now he's just a theory to them." He smiled wickedly. "Tomorrow he will become reality."

She frowned, shaking her head in despair over his attitude. "What do you think he'll do?"

"Oh, I don't know. Climb out on a precipice and hang by his knees until they have to employ a helicopter to get him back. Set the horses free from the stables. Put piranhas in the moat. Or maybe they have a nice wedding cake he could ruin."

She clenched her hands together distractedly. "Does it ever occur to you that he does these things because you expect him to?"

He sighed. "There's a background here, Elena. I expect these things because he's done them before."

She licked her dry lips. She was developing such an interest in this man, and yet there were so many things about him that would normally turn her away. But she couldn't dismiss him now. She was experiencing emotions she'd never had before and that meant she had to stay with him, try to understand—or, even better, try to help *him* understand and change. Was that crazy? Was she being arrogant herself? Was she chasing fireflies?

Probably. But it was too late to quit now. She was in for the duration—whatever that turned out to be.

"If he really is as bad as you say, aren't you afraid taking him to the palace could make them think twice about accepting you as King? After all, he would come with the deal, from their point of view."

Adam thought about that. "You've got a point there. Maybe I won't take him over until the ink is dry."

She took a deep breath, closed her eyes and plunged in. "Adam, don't you think this idea of becoming King could use a little more thought? Maybe it's just not right for you."

"What?" He wasn't sure he'd heard her right. Every part of his body reacted with shock. "What are you talking about?"

Her hands were clenched so tightly, the knuckles were white. "Just this, Adam. What makes you think you're right for the job? What makes you think you'll be a good king?"

"A good king?" His laugh was short, cold and dismissive. "What does that have to do with anything?"

"It's the basis of everything," she said earnestly. "If you can't be a good king, why would you want the job?"

"The 'job'?" He stared at her, swore softly, and began pacing as well. "It's not the 'job' I want, Elena. It's the compensation for the job. I've already got a job. I run a film production company and I'm damn good at it." He raked his fingers through his thick hair. "My company has been everything to me for years. I'll do anything to keep from losing it." He stopped in front of her. "Including play around at being King if that's what I have to do."

That was exactly what she'd feared. She turned from him. It was tempting to let it go. After all, what made her think she could change anything? And if she confronted him, told him what she really thought, he might decide she wasn't worth the effort. And much as she kept telling herself she'd been fine before she knew him and she would be fine if he walked out on her tonight, she knew it wasn't true. He'd already changed her life. And she didn't want to lose him—not yet, at any rate.

But she couldn't live a lie, either. And her first responsibility was to her island, to her people, to all those ancestors hanging around at the ruins. So she gathered her courage and turned back to face him.

"Adam, I've thought about this all afternoon. And I have to tell you what I think." She drew in a full breath and let it out. "You should withdraw your name from consideration."

"What?"

"You can't be King of Niroli."

CHAPTER SIX

"You have to withdraw, Adam," Elena said, her voice quivering with emotion. "It's just not right. You'd be a terrible king."

Adam stared at her, appalled. Why was it that the women in his life always turned on him? "What are you talking about? I thought you were on my side."

She heard the tight thread of emotion in his voice and knew she'd cut him to the quick. But she had to be honest. She couldn't back down now.

"I *am* on your side. I'm on the side of you doing what's right and not cheating people."

He couldn't believe she was saying these things. He reached out to take her shoulders in his hands, but he stopped himself just in time and pulled back, spinning on his heel instead and slamming a fist into a pillow on the back of the couch.

"Elena, I'm not cheating anyone. They're desperate for a king. I can be King. I've got the genes for it. I didn't ask for this choice. They're the ones who asked me to come."

Fabio had raised his head as the argument began. Now he rose and moved quietly to stand in front of Elena. Adam looked at that and wanted to laugh. Even the dog had turned on him.

"Let them choose someone else," Elena said, standing tough, though her lower lip was trembling. "Please, Adam. For your own good."

"That's just it, Elena. I don't think there is anyone else. I'm it. It's the end of the line for them. That's why I hope to get a lot out of this deal."

Money again. Always the money. She shook her head, because she knew he wasn't the only one. She'd let him stay here for the money. How could she criticize him? Still, she had to try to make him see that taking this position would only end up ruining him.

"If you are the end of the line, a new line should be started. There are many noble families. You read about them all the time. Let them choose one and start a new dynasty. Perhaps bring in a royal from another country. Other countries have done that in the past." She threw up her hands and a tremor of emotion entered her voice. "But it must be someone who appreciates Niroli and loves us. Someone who lives and breathes the Nirolian spirit."

"The Nirolian spirit," he repeated, pained, shaking his head, and his tone was sarcastic. "What exactly is the Nirolian spirit?"

"You don't know and that's why you can't be King. You have to live and breathe it. You can't phone it in from Hollywood."

His head went back as though she'd slapped him.

Something in her words and the way she said them stung like nothing had in a long time. He knew he couldn't refute her logic. The thing was, he didn't care about the things she thought were so important. He didn't want to care.

But he didn't like being seen as a cad, either. Especially by this woman he was learning to admire so much. And since he had no answer, he turned on his heel and left the room.

"Adam?"

Adam stretched and smiled.

"Adam?"

Her hand was on his shoulder and he turned, reaching for her. She was soft and smooth and rounded, just as he'd known she would be, and her body was like heaven against his as he…

"Adam! Stop! Wake up!"

"What?" He blinked at her groggily and wondered why she was looming over him in the dark instead of being down here in bed alongside him where she belonged.

"I couldn't sleep," she was whispering. "Please come outside. I've got to talk to you and I don't want to wake Jeremy."

"Yeah. Okay. Uh…just give me a minute here." He shook his head. "Wow. I thought I was dreaming."

"I'll wait for you outside."

"Yeah. I'll be there in a second."

He took a deep breath to steady himself. That dream had been a little too real. Rolling off the bed, he checked his son, then went out to meet Elena. She was standing at the side of the yard under a spreading tree where a small waterfall spilled into a tiny pond. The sound of the water seemed to fill the yard with music.

"What's the matter?" he asked her, not yet clear on why she'd wakened him. "Is something wrong?"

"Yes," she said. "*I'm* wrong."

"What?"

Stretching, he rubbed the top of his head with his palm and yawned. He was wearing nothing but pajama bottoms, but that hardly mattered, since she couldn't see him. At least that was what he was telling himself. In reality, he knew very well that his naked torso and the loose pants hanging low on his hips made him feel more sensually aware than ever. Already his body was reacting to the cool breeze against his naked skin—and the ethereal look of the woman before him in the moonlight.

Elena's hair was floating around her face and she had on some white lacy thing with another white lacy thing over it, making him want to rip into all that beautiful lace and open her up like a midnight present. He had a quick vision of what that would look like and sucked in his breath sharply. But then he grimaced and shook his head. He was dreaming again.

"Why are you wrong?" he asked instead of pursuing the fantasy.

"I shouldn't have said the things I did to you. It's really not my business to try to tell you what to do. And I wanted you to know that I'm sorry."

"You're sorry."

He frowned, trying to remember what she'd said exactly. It had been all about him not being worthy of being King. That didn't mean he was going to give up the position. But she wasn't wrong. She'd been so right, he hadn't been able to mount a decent defense of his actions. But that was just it. He actually was opportunistic, money-grubbing scum and he knew it. The problem being, there was no cure.

"I was wrong," she was insisting. "You shouldn't give up on being King because you don't love Niroli enough. I was coming at it from the wrong angle. And I have an idea." Her face was turned up and she looked completely sincere—and so darn beautiful, he just wanted to take her in his arms and begin kissing her all over. But she was so earnest, he forced himself to listen to what she had to say instead.

"Here it is." She pointed a finger at his chest. "What you need to do is to start loving Niroli."

He considered that for a second or two before nodding. "Okay." He shrugged, ready to please. "How do I do that?"

Her smile was impish in the moonlight. "I've got a plan."

He smiled back at her, aching to kiss those red lips, leaning toward her as though she were a magnet. Her cover-all had slipped off her shoulder, exposing the fact that her beautiful breasts were bra-less and swaying free before him. He'd never seen flesh that looked so inviting. His throat thickened with desire, but he managed to croak out, "That sounds ominous."

"No," she said earnestly. Excitement for her idea fairly bounced off her. "It's a good plan. Tomorrow when you have some time, I'm going to take you out and show you Niroli. Gino was right. You need to do some sightseeing."

He pulled back, frowning. Mentioning Gino tended to throw cold water on his libido every time. "Let me get this straight. The blind lady is going to take me out to see the sights."

"Why not?" She laughed up at him.

Why not indeed? Anything the blind lady wanted…

He stretched his hands out just inches from her. He didn't dare touch her, but he got as close as he could. Close enough to catch her spicy scent. Close enough to feel the heat from her perfect body. Close enough so that a strand of her hair tickled his face while another set up a series of sensations as it danced against his naked chest.

"Well, what do you think?" she was asking.

He could hardly talk. His body was throbbing with an urgent and ancient need to join with hers.

"Uh…sounds great," he rasped out.

"Good. 'Til tomorrow, then."

"Goodnight."

"Goodnight."

She'd almost turned to go back into the house, but she hesitated, and suddenly he was watching in surprise as her hand snaked out and reached for him. It flattened high against his chest, feeling hot against his cool skin. He heard her quick, sharp gasp, and then her mouth opened in soundless wonder as her hand traveled slowly down the length of his abdomen, the palm rubbing an exquisite path of exploration and sensation, the fingers lightly trailing, until it reached his navel.

"Oh, my," she whispered, then drew back quickly, turned on a dime, and was gone.

Adam stood where he was, unable to move, for a long, long time.

Adam went for a good long run as soon as he woke in the morning. When he got back, Elena had prepared a savory frittata and baked some tiny cinnamon rolls to go with it. Jeremy was at the piano, singing and pretending to play at the same time, but he stopped as soon as he saw his father arrive.

Par for the course, Adam thought bleakly. The kid just didn't much want him around.

"You missed Gino," Elena sang out when she realized Adam was in the room. "He said to give you his very best."

"His best what?" he grumbled, sniffing the air and appreciating the cooking smells. "His best knuckle sandwich?"

"Now now," she said, chuckling. She was taking a bit of guilty pleasure in having a couple of men tussle over her, even if it was on a very superficial level. "Gino wants what's best for me."

"Sure he does. The only trouble is, he thinks *he's* what's best for you. And he's wrong."

Really? And how do you know that, mister? Elena tossed back her hair and said aloud, "I'm serving breakfast in the yard in about fifteen minutes. Come on out if you're hungry."

"Great," he responded. "Mind if I take a shower first?"

"Of course not. Go right ahead. Fresh towels are in the cabinet in the corner."

"Thanks."

She listened as he walked down the hall and disappeared into the bathroom. She was smiling again. Why was she catching herself smiling all the time? But there was no point in asking that question. She knew exactly why.

"I've got a silly crush," she told herself softly. "And that's all it is."

Hopefully, it would be fun while it lasted. Because dreaming that it could possibly be anything serious would be evidence of a grave mental illness and she knew it. But whenever she let herself think about how his flesh had felt beneath her hand out in the midnight garden, she couldn't catch her breath for a moment and then she felt butterflies swarming all through her system. That was something she'd never felt before. And it was pretty darn delicious.

This was almost like a romance. And she'd never had a real live romance before. It was only now that she was beginning to understand how very protected she'd always been. So she was going to enjoy this little pretend romance. Nothing too serious. In fact, she was going to call it a learning experience.

She knew she was at a disadvantage because of her blindness. She had to try to piece together his reactions, because she couldn't see the look in his eyes. Had he liked it when she'd touched him? She thought so, but she couldn't be sure. Sometimes you just had to go on faith.

At least she was pretty sure he hadn't hated it. He hadn't pulled away, and she thought she'd heard his breathing go a bit ragged. Her heart had been beating so hard, though, it had been difficult to hear anything else.

Yes, all in all, she was glad she'd followed her instincts and done it. Now all she could think about was— when could she get a chance to do it again?

She went ahead and fed Jeremy while Adam was showering, then let him run off to play with Fabio while she set out place mats on the little wrought-iron table in her yard. When Adam came out, smelling of soap and shampoo, and bristling with freshness, she was ready.

"Wow," he said. "This looks great. And I'm starving."

She poured him some orange juice, then his coffee. He tried everything but liked the cinnamon rolls best. "I could eat a dozen of these," he admitted. "They're great. And you baked them yourself. Is there anything you can't do?"

She didn't reply. She hated compliments, which always contained the implied "well done considering…" After making sure he had everything he needed, she sat down across from him and leaned her face in her hands.

"Adam, something has been bothering me."

He looked up from eating and smiled at the picture she made with her pretty face framed that way. "What's that?"

"Last night when I was ranting at you, I was so wrapped up in my concern as to whether you should be

King that I hardly noticed something you said. Later, it came back to me and I realized it was so much more important than what I was going on and on about."

He went still. "What are you talking about?"

She pressed her lips together, listening to make sure Jeremy and Fabio were far enough away, then let it out in a rush. "What you said about Jeremy. That you didn't think he cared about you."

He sighed. "Ah. My moment of clarity."

The bitterness in his voice was a confirmation of her theories. "Not clarity. Resentment, maybe. Pain, certainly. But so blockheaded!"

That put his shoulders back a bit and he reacted with some defensiveness. "I think I know my son better than you do. And I've come to the conclusion, after long, careful analysis, that he doesn't like me much." He took a long sip of coffee.

"Adam, that is just insane," she insisted ardently. "He adores you."

He shook his head, rejecting that out of hand. It would be nice to let himself believe that, but he had gone too long trying to pretend this was just a phase and Jeremy would grow out of it. He was tired of faking it—especially with Elena. Somehow she had very quickly become the one person in the world he felt he couldn't fool.

"Elena, please. That just doesn't work. I know what you're doing, and the fact that you feel you have to do it only makes things worse."

Elena wished with all her heart she knew the right words to say to convince him of how wrong he was.

How did she know? That was the problem. She couldn't have said for sure.

"Adam, your son loves you. He cares desperately about what you think of him. He just doesn't know how to show you."

He wiped his mouth with his napkin and threw it down on the table. "You're the one who's dreaming now. Maybe it's because you can't see the way he looks at me."

She drew back and he swore softly once he realized what he'd done. He'd used her blindness against her in an argument. That was a lousy thing to do and he vowed right then and there that he was never going to do it again.

But it didn't stop her from responding quickly. "No, I can't see him, but I can hear the way he talks about you when you're not there." She shook her head. "Adam, you're just wrong and I'm going to find a way to prove it to you."

He lingered at the table, touched that she felt so strongly about this but sure that she was the one who was wrong. After all, he'd lived with it for years and she'd only seen Jeremy for the last two days. And he'd been on his best behavior around her. She just didn't have a clue.

Still, the fact that the kid acted as he did was probably Adam's fault from the beginning.

"I don't know, Elena," he said slowly. "I never had a father. Maybe I just don't know how to be one. Maybe that's the root of the whole problem."

"Your mother never married anyone else?"

His chuckle was humorless. "My mother never was

the marrying kind," he said, his light tone belying the seriousness of the subject. "She's had a long and very successful career as a party girl. I was raised by a loving grandmother and a grandfather who was a gruff old man who mostly glowered and growled, until he had a stroke when I was about eight."

Elena shook her head, puzzled. "So, where was your mother?"

"Busy. Dating. Partying. Modeling for a few years. And when that dried up, she became a professional party person."

Elena frowned, appalled. "How do you make a living doing that?"

He grunted. "If you have to ask, you don't want to know."

"Oh." She blinked, still not sure she understood but willing to leave it at that. "And she still can survive that way?"

"She's still a very beautiful woman. It's a sad imitation of a real life she leads, but it's hers and she's used to it."

She didn't hear any bitterness in his voice and that bewildered her. Here this woman had abandoned him from a very early age, left him to the kindness of grandparents who probably would rather have lived their retirement years in peace and quiet—and he didn't seem to care.

"Don't you resent her and the way she behaved?"

He didn't answer for a long moment and she began to wonder if she'd offended him. But once he did respond, she could tell he'd just been thinking it over.

"I've resented her from time to time. But I'm a little

old to be blaming all my misfortunes on my poor little mother." He hesitated, then went on. "The sad thing is that Melissa, Jeremy's birth mother, is driven in a similar way. She thinks having a film career is going to make her happy. She'll give up everything for it. And once she gets what she thinks she wants…it will taste like ashes in her mouth."

Her instincts told her he was probably being quite perceptive, but she wondered what in his experience had given him such wisdom. "How do you know that?"

"I've been around the business for years and years. I've seen it all play out time after time. So many of these people basically sell their soul to the devil. And at some time, the devil wants his due." His smile was bitter-sweet. "Not to get too fanciful about it, but it really does seem to play out that way. I only wish I could have convinced Melissa. But she was obsessed. She had to have it."

Now she could hear bitterness. He couldn't forgive Melissa the way he could forgive his mother. She had a quick intuition that his deep paternal feelings for Jeremy were tied in to that.

He rose and went into the house to try to make a few calls to California. She sat where she was and wished she could make everyone happy with magic—or a wise word or two. She felt helpless. Helpless—and blind. Suddenly, achingly, she wanted to see so badly, it over-whelmed her. If she could only see, maybe she would be able to find a way to fix things for the people she loved. Maybe she would be smarter, more perceptive.

The way would be clear and she could charge ahead, secure and full of righteous energy.

But, even more, if she could only see Adam's beautiful face. She longed to see it, to really know him, to carry his image in her heart and her memory. The horrible truth was, she would never be able to do that. And for just a moment, tears filled her sightless eyes.

She wiped them quickly, and after a few shuddering breaths she calmed herself and began to return to normal. By the time she heard Adam coming back, she was herself again. And he sounded as though either his calls had been successful, or he had decided to push all that to the back of his mind for a few hours and banish unhappiness for the rest of the day.

"This weather is great," he said, dropping back into his chair. "Are we still on for today?"

"Yes." She hesitated, hiding her wet napkin in her lap. "When do you plan to go to the palace?"

He stretched back in his chair and looked at her. What was it about this woman that had so captured his imagination? Memories of what had happened the night before kept surfacing. Even a good hard run hadn't wrung the lingering throb of desire out of his system. When she'd touched him, let her hand run down his naked form from chest to navel, he'd thought his heart would stop. No woman had ever done anything sexier to him.

The sensuality had been even more intense because he'd known she was doing it so innocently. And he knew he couldn't let himself reciprocate. She was a forever sort of girl, and he was about to be King. The two didn't match and, for once in his life, he was going to do what was right instead of what felt good. He was going to keep his hands off her.

She looked so appealing, sitting there in the morning sunlight. He wanted her more than he'd ever wanted a woman before. But he couldn't have her that way. Still, he wanted to be with her now as much as possible, while he still could be.

"They want me there at noon," he said at last. "But you know what? I think I'll skip the palace today. I'd rather go sightseeing with you. And my not showing up might light a fire under them. Who knows?"

"Oh." Her smile was radiant. "Well, good."

He basked in it. "So what's the plan?"

"Well, unless you object, I've made arrangements for Jeremy to play with Tommy, the little boy next door who is just his age. You met his parents last night…Lisa and her husband Ted."

"Sounds great, as long as they're prepared for mayhem."

She was shocked every time he said these things. "Adam! He hasn't done anything since he's been here."

"You wait."

She started to protest again, then held her tongue. This sort of argument wouldn't get either one of them anywhere.

"So how are we going to do this? You don't have a car." His eyebrows rose as it occurred to him she did all sorts of things he didn't expect. "Do you?" he asked, aghast at the thought.

She laughed. "No, I haven't tried driving. But I do know someone who can drive us."

"Who is it?"

"Gino usually gives me a ride when I need one, but he's busy today. But he's got a cousin named Louie who has a car and he said he'd send him over—"

"Aha. A spy."

"What are you talking about?"

He grinned, recognizing motives. "Gino wants to keep an eye on us."

"Oh, Adam… "

"But I've got a better idea. When I was running this morning, I saw a place where they rent out Vespas."

Her mouth dropped open. "Vespas!"

"Yeah. They look like a lot of fun. We can get one big enough for two."

"But…but what about Fabio?"

Adam grinned. "Can't you just see him hanging on for dear life with his ears flapping in the wind?"

"No, I can't!"

"Oh. Of course not." He touched her hand and drew back quickly. "We'll have to leave him with Jeremy."

"But…" Suddenly she didn't feel so brave. Didn't he understand how naked and alone she would be out in unfamiliar territory without Fabio? "I need Fabio. All my independence is based on Fabio."

"You won't need Fabio. You'll have me." His voice lowered. "Don't you trust me to keep you safe?"

"Yes," she said, tentatively at first, then with strong conviction. "Yes, I do trust you."

"Okay, then. It'll be an adventure for both of us."

She cocked her head to the side. "Why for you?"

He grinned. "I've never driven a Vespa before."

"Oh, no!"

"You and me on a Vespa. It's perfect, because the paparazzi will never connect us with the pair they're looking for—he who would be King and the blind piano player he's hanging out with."

"Perfect," she echoed. And for the moment, it was. Excitement tingled every nerve she owned.

CHAPTER SEVEN

DRIVING a Vespa was a piece of cake. At least, that was what Adam told himself, and, in truth, he did pretty well right from the beginning. But that didn't stop Elena from shrieking a bit and holding on very tightly.

That holding on thing was fine with him. She could do that all day—and, actually, that was pretty much the plan. So he was a happy man as they did a few practice runs up and down the main drag of Monte Speziare. Looking out at the people on the street and the local shopkeepers, he could see what Elena couldn't—that the whole town seemed to be coming out to watch Elena ride off on a Vespa with a stranger. It was evident that everyone knew her. There was much pointing and laughing and calling out with good wishes, as though everyone was invested in seeing Elena get out in the world and have a good time. But Elena was intent on just staying alive and she missed most of it.

"Here we go," he called back to her, and they took off down the highway, racing past the turnoff to the Roman ruins where they'd met and heading down the coast. They'd packed swimsuits and towels, a basket of snacks and an ice bag of cold drinks, all slung in saddle-bags, all preparations for their adventure. The weather was perfect. All systems were go.

It took Elena a few minutes to stabilize. At first, she could barely breathe with the wind whipping in her face. She felt as though she were hurtling through space. It was pretty scary. Luckily, she had a big strong man to hang onto.

And that was the best part. Once she caught her breath and settled down, she began to enjoy the hard, muscular body she was going to cling to for the better part of the day. He was a solid piece of reality to anchor this fantasy-like experience. What could be better?

"Where are we?" she called out.

"The sign says we're about to go past the Roman Amphitheater," he told her.

"Oh, pull off. You must see the amphitheater."

He pulled off and zoomed into the parking lot, where they parked and got off to walk to the huge and very ancient amphitheater, built by the Romans cen-turies before.

"There are performances given here to this day," she told him. "I attended a presentation of *Aida* here last summer."

"That's incredible when you stop to think about it," Adam said, mulling over the historical ramifications. "Think of all the old ghosts hanging around."

She laughed. "The place must be getting pretty crowded," she agreed.

The next few hours were filled with similar experiences. They swooped past castle after castle, then stopped on the cliff road overlooking the old port, giving a panoramic view of the ships coming into the harbor and the sailboats heading out for a day of touring. A huge cruise ship was just departing, making its slow, deliberate way out to sea. With the sunlight sparkling on the water, the view was majestic and Adam had to admit it gave him a sense of the grandeur of the island and its place in the world.

"Tell me what you see," she prodded quietly. "This is the one thing that leaves me at a disadvantage. I need some clues. Give me your vision."

He stumbled over the task at first, wanting to get it right for her but hesitant. Still, he got better as they went along, and very soon it became automatic. Eventually, he began to color his straight-up descriptions with his own emotional reactions, making them more and more relevant. Elena had never felt her hunger for sight so filled with true vision.

"You are a treasure," she murmured at one point.

"What?" he said, craning back to look at her.

"Nothing," she said, patting his shoulder and smiling at him. "Carry on, driver."

"Yes, madam," he said, playing along.

They travelled on down the coast past where the lovely city of Porto di Castellante nestled into the hills above the main port, then headed inland to glide between the vineyards spread out in neat rows for miles, and the orchards of olive trees and bright patches of orange groves. The mountains in the background made for spectacular scenery.

"I'd take you up into the foothills," she teased him, "but they are full of bandits. We might have to fight our way back out again."

They turned south instead, driving past extinct volcanoes and turning up toward the new tourist area where the beaches were long and lovely and filled with golden sand and the new luxury hotels and casinos seemed to be growing and expanding before their eyes. Everything was new and clean and luxurious. They stopped for lunch at a small roadside café, just off the beaten path of tourist bustle, but close enough to catch a hint of the excitement.

"You're winning me over," Adam admitted as they toasted their adventure with glasses of a local vintage. "This island is one of the most beautiful places I've ever been."

"Of course," Elena said, leaning forward. "But are you beginning to feel connected to it? Does it bring up genetic memories? Do you 'feel the vibes'?"

He thought for a moment. "I think so," he said. "I'll let you know by the end of the day. After I've taken in everything and synthesized it."

"You'll feel it," she said confidently. "You have Niroli blood in your veins. You can thank your father for that." She paused, hesitating a moment, wondering if he would mind her next question. But she had to ask it.

"Adam…did you ever meet your father?"

He drew in a sharp breath as though the question surprised him, but he didn't hesitate to answer it. "No. But I saw him once."

"You did?"

"I was sixteen. My mother thought it would be cute to take her teenage son along to Rome for the spring party season. It wasn't long before she put me on a plane for home, but while it lasted it was a great experience. And one day I was shopping with one of her friends and a big black limousine came up, escorted by flanks of motorcycle officers. My mother's friend pointed to the man getting out of the car. 'There's your father,' she said. 'That's the Crown Prince of Niroli.'"

"Had you seen a picture of him before that?"

"Sure. My mother had pictures. But he'd always seemed more like a movie star, something remote. So to see him in person…" He stopped for a moment and cleared his throat.

"I started following him. It was like I was possessed. I had to get closer, so I followed him into the department store and then from floor to floor. Very soon his security guards began to notice me and they quickly barred me from the area. But before they did, he turned suddenly and we came face to face."

"Did you say anything?"

"No. But I think he knew who I was. I felt like there was a connection there. He stared at me and a look came over his face…" To his surprise, a lump suddenly appeared in his throat and he coughed to get rid of it.

"When I was about eighteen I wrote him a letter. I got a form letter back. 'Thank you for your correspon-

dence, but the prince does not answer personal letters.'
So much for that."

Elena ached for him. Reaching out, she found his
hand and covered it with hers, wishing she knew something she could do.

"That was why I was bound and determined to take
care of Jeremy," he went on. "When Melissa walked out,
she told me…" he laughed, but there was nothing
amusing about the sound of it "…she told me to put him
up for adoption. Like a puppy. Like a pet rabbit." He
sucked in his breath. "He was so little and so helpless.
He needed…someone. I thought it could be me." His
voice deepened with doubt. "Now I'm not so sure.
Maybe I was the selfish one. Maybe he would have
been better off being adopted by some nice couple."

Elena's heart broke for him. She knew it wasn't easy
for him to tell her all this, but at the same time she was
glad to hear it. Knowing this about Adam made her
feelings for him seem vindicated.

"Adoption can be a wonderful thing," she murmured.
"But so can fatherhood."

He frowned, realizing suddenly that his self-absorbed
mood was raining on this celebratory parade. "How
about you, Elena?" he asked. "I've never heard anything
about your father."

She looked surprised at his interest, but the question
didn't bother her.

"My father disappeared when I was a little girl," she
said with a matter-of-fact tone that had to belie its im-
portance in her life. "Right around the time I went blind.

I always assumed it was because he couldn't handle it. My mother insisted that wasn't true, but, with a little girl's intuition, I knew it was."

"And you've heard nothing about him since?"

"Not a thing. I have no idea what happened to him. And at this point, I really don't care."

He stared at her. "Now there, you see?" he said at last. "Your past is just as screwed up as mine is. How come we're always talking about mine and not yours?"

She laughed softly. "Because you, my fine feathered friend, are about to become King of Niroli. You count. I don't."

"Oh, no, Elena," he said, grabbing her hand again and holding it tightly. "That's where you're wrong. You are quickly becoming one of the people who counts the most. At least in my life."

Her heart jumped, but she wondered what he really meant and why he would say such a thing. There could be nothing meaningful between them. Her harmless little crush on him was one thing. For him to encourage her to hope for something more was asking for disaster. So what was his reason?

Whatever it was would have to wait for awhile. The waiter arrived with their meal and the talk turned back to their tour of the island. An hour later, they were on the road again, this time heading for the spa that Elena's friend Natalia ran out on the coast.

"She uses the special mud from the volcanoes," Elena told Adam. "It's wonderful. You'll have to try it sometime."

They left the Vespa in the parking lot and had a tour

of the spa, though Natalia wasn't there. As they left Elena heard a familiar voice in the parking lot.

"Elena!" someone was calling. "Hello, dear, it's Susan."

"Susan!" Elena turned, delighted to greet her mother's friend Susan Nablus. And then she realized she was going to have to introduce her. Was she going to claim the man with her wasn't who he really was? She knew very well Susan would never believe it. But the decision was quickly taken out of her hands.

"Adam Ryder," Susan was saying, putting two and two together and drawing the obvious conclusion. "Oh, my goodness, it's an honor to meet you, sir." And she did a modified curtsy right there in the parking lot.

"Hey, hey, none of that," Adam said jokingly. "I'm just plain old Rex Burbank at this point."

Susan looked perplexed and Elena explained to Adam who Susan was, then explained about the Rex Burbank name to Susan.

"Soon it will be 'Your Majesty'," Susan said, laughing. "And there will be no doubt."

"Hmm—I could get used to that," Adam admitted.

"Susan is a historian," Elena told him. "Her concentration is in the history of our island country. If you want to know anything about the past, you should consult her."

"Good to know."

"Yes," Susan said. "I give a seminar on Nirolian history. Once you've been installed as King, I would be glad to come to the palace and give my presentation to you, or any of your retinue."

"My retinue?" He grinned. "Thanks. That sounds like something I will definitely want to do."

"Such luck to have met you here," Susan went on happily after they had told her all about their tour and showed her the Vespa. "You see, I've just been awarded the contract to write the official biography of your father, Crown Prince Antonio."

Elena gasped. "Seriously?"

"Yes. I'm very excited about it. And I wonder if I could…if it would be possible…well, to impose on you for an interview."

"Me?" Adam was shocked. "What do I have to do with him?"

"You're his son. And soon to take the place he would have taken, had he lived."

Adam shook his head slowly, his eyes troubled. "I don't see how I would figure into his story at all."

Susan disagreed. "You must have a unique perspective on things."

"I doubt it. My father and I never had any contact. It's possible he never knew I existed." Adam shook his head and looked firm. "I'm sorry but I'd rather not get involved in something like that. I just wouldn't feel comfortable about it."

Susan looked as if she had more arguments in her arsenal, but it was obvious the two of them were anxious to get back to their tour and she decided to table them for now.

"Well, there will be plenty of time if you should change your mind," she said, watching them get back on the Vespa. "I'll probably be working on this for years."

She waved as they drove off, then started back toward the spa steps. Elena hugged herself to Adam's back and closed her eyes, glad to have him to herself again.

As they headed back up the coast Adam saw the royal palace in the distance. It seemed like a sign that this idyllic day was just about over and he was going to have to go back to thinking about becoming a king. But this was something Elena had given him, something he hadn't had before—a sense of what being King of Niroli was all about.

There was one last place he'd heard about that he wanted to try, and when he saw the sign for the Raining Rapids Water Slide, he turned the Vespa and headed that way.

"We're doing what?" Elena cried when he told her where they were stopping.

"We're going down the water slide. Haven't you ever been?"

"No. I don't think I can do that kind of thing."

He was surprised. "Elena, I thought you could do just about anything."

"I can," she said stoutly. "Anything except this."

"But this isn't half as scary as the traffic you walk out into every day."

She pressed her lips together, worried. "I don't know."

He took her hand and tugged on it. "Come on. We brought the swim suits and everything."

"I thought we were going swimming at the beach."

"That's scarier than this. There aren't any sharks on a water slide."

She still hung back. She could hear other people gathering, calling back and forth and preparing for the ride, and she could hear the screams of people going down the slide. They were happy screams, but screams none the less. Her mouth was a little dry.

"Adam, I'm not sure. How high is it? I just don't have any experience with something like this. I don't know how to guard against…"

"I'll be with you."

She turned her face up toward his. "How can you be with me? I'll be sliding down a huge water slide built into the rock…"

"I'll be with you every inch of the way. I'll hold you."

She stopped dead. "You'll…you'll hold me?"

"Yes."

She tightened her grip on his hand. "You won't let go?"

He brought her hand up to his lips and kissed it. "I swear, Elena," he said, his voice deep and resonant. "I won't let you go."

She swallowed hard. "Well, okay, then."

He grinned. "Come on."

They changed into suits in the dressing rooms, then climbed to the top of the structure built into the solid limestone on the mountain. Adam held her hand and she leaned into him whenever she could. Her heart was thumping in her chest. She could hear the joyful screams as people went sailing down into the mist.

Easy for them to be excited—they could see where they were going! She was brave and she'd trained herself to do a lot of things people didn't expect, but new risks were always scary. She didn't want to get hurt, of course. But, even more than that, she didn't want to look bumbling and foolish in front of Adam. That scared her most of all.

And finally it was their turn. Adam took their piece of plastic, sat down on it and pulled her down before him and between his legs. He held her tightly and she leaned back against him. The gush of water came, and they were off. It went very fast, but the sensation was spectacular. Racing the wind, slicing through water, taking the turn and then down into the flume. Elena was screaming and laughing at the same time. Adam's arms were holding her safe and his legs were holding her in the cradle of his hips and it felt very sexy. As they landed, laughing at the finish, she wasn't sure which was more thrilling—the ride or Adam's obvious reaction to holding her.

"Did you like it?" he asked as they struggled up and began to walk away.

"I loved it," she told him honestly. "I want to do it again."

"On your own this time?"

"No. Oh, no!" She laughed up at him mischievously. "Having you hold me is the best part of the ride."

He laughed back. She was so darn honest!

"Okay," he said, grabbing her hand. "Let's go again."

* * *

They were both tired when they got back to the cottage—tired and happy. Gino was waiting for them. He was tired, too, but he wasn't happy.

"If this keeps up, I'm going to have to buy you a cell phone," he said crossly. "You were incommunicado for the entire day!"

"I don't need a cell phone," she protested.

"You don't have a cell phone?" Adam said, surprised. "How do you manage without one?"

"I don't need one. I don't really have anyone to call."

He didn't believe that for a moment. Most women he knew lived with a cell permanently attached to their ear.

"You could call *me*," he suggested. "Then at least I'd have someone on the other end of the line once in awhile."

Gino frowned fiercely. "I'm the one she needs to call," he said. "And maybe *Rex* here ought to leave his number with someone when he takes you off so you could be found."

"Oh, Gino, we weren't lost," she responded, still too happy from the day to get annoyed with him. "Just gone for a bit."

"Right. And in the meantime, here's a letter from the New York School. It came in your mail today. For all you know, they might need an immediate answer." He waved an envelope in the air.

"Oh! Read it to me, quickly. What do they say?"

Gino made a show of dramatically opening the envelope, glaring at Adam all the time.

"'Dear Miss Valerio,'" he began, then smiled at Elena. "You see, it's not a form letter."

"Just read!" she said.

He nodded and got back to it. "'We are very pleased to inform you that after convening a special meeting to consider your situation as explained to us by a communication from Mr Gino Scallerri, we have the following proposal to make.'"

Gino went on reading as Elena sat listening with her mouth open in astonishment. It seemed that Gino had written to the scholarship committee at the school, explaining Elena's rare ability to deal with her blindness, and describing her state of poverty, which made it impossible for her to accept the scholarship she'd been awarded. The committee had found funds and were offering her a grant that would make it possible for her to come to New York and stay in a group home for the next six months in order to study music therapy.

"Exactly what you need in order to go," Gino crowed. "Did I do good? Didn't I tell you to be patient?"

"Oh, Gino!" She threw herself into his arms and they danced about the room, laughing and celebrating.

Adam watched. He was happy for Elena. From what she'd said, he knew this was just what she'd been hoping for. But at the same time he didn't relish the thought of losing her right after he'd discovered how wonderful she was. And he wasn't crazy about it being Gino who had engineered the windfall.

But Elena was happy. That was the most important thing.

He slipped away to go next door and get his son and Fabio while she and Gino made plans. Checking his messages, he had more evidence that his business was in dire trouble, and a few anxious phone calls from the palace. It seemed the "important" people had returned, and he was going to have to go in to see them this evening after all.

There was a new, apprehensive feeling in the pit of his stomach. There was an oddly tense tone to the calls from the royal committee. Something told him the news there would not be all good and he'd better be prepared for anything.

CHAPTER EIGHT

ADAM had been in Niroli for almost a week and the final papers were still unsigned. The meetings at the palace had become longer and more tedious. He'd been presented with non-negotiable rule after non-negotiable rule and he was beginning to wonder if he would be able to meet their expectations. He'd always known he would have to walk a fine line on a few of their demands, but when they came up with things such as, "The ruler of Niroli must dedicate his life to the Kingdom. Therefore he is not permitted to have a profession", and "The ruler can give permission for Royal House members to live elsewhere, but the ruler must reside in Niroli" and they actually seemed to mean it, he got a bit uneasy about his ability to game this system.

Could he actually do this thing? Hell, he had to. And soon, or saving his production company would be a moot point. Zeb was on the phone to him every day, and every day they came another step closer to losing control of the company. There was almost no time left. If something didn't happen in the next few days, his company, the foundation of his whole sense of worth, the only thing he'd ever done right with his life, would be no more. He was jittery and edgy and about to go off the deep end. Something had to give.

The saving grace in his life right now was Elena. She'd worked wonders with Jeremy and she was such a calming influence in his own life that he felt himself more and more eager to get back to her every day. And the irony was, the king's counselors were pushing hard for him to move to the palace and leave Elena behind. The media had found out about his hiding place and there had been articles in the local papers. The palace read the papers just like everyone else. And they didn't much like what they'd read.

"We must insist that you begin meeting suitable women for consideration as your queen right away," was the way Tours had put it. "Blind piano teachers are not in the running."

That had put Adam's back up but he'd managed to hold his temper, though he had told Tours pretty much what he could do with his candidates for Queen. Still, he'd agreed to making the move to other quarters by the beginning of the next week. Elena would be gone by then anyway.

Elena was going to New York. All the details had been worked out and she was rushing around getting ready to close up her house and head for her new studies at the New York School of Music Applications. She still found time to work with Jeremy and from the amazing transformation she'd made there, it was pretty obvious she was a natural at it. Jeremy was playing actual pieces on the piano and his attitude toward life was completely different from what it had been just days before. Adam had the feeling that Elena would end up teaching the experts a thing or two before she was through.

Jeremy's seventh birthday had landed right in the middle of their visit two days before. When Elena had found out about it, she had immediately begun planning a party, despite being overwhelmed by preparations for her move to New York.

"He doesn't need a party," Adam had told her when he'd heard. "Give him a new computer game or an hour at a video parlor. Get him a pizza. That's all he wants."

"You see, that's where you're wrong," she told him carefully. "That is what he may say he wants. That actually may be what he *thinks* he wants. But it is not what he really wants."

"Oh, yeah? And you know better." He threw up his hands. "But what am I saying? Of course you know better. So tell me, Elena. What does he really want?"

"Signs of love and esteem. And that is why we are having the party. We have to show him that we care enough to go out of our way to do this for him."

He scoffed at the time, but she was right. Jeremy loved his party. She decorated the place with balloons and streamers and brought in a huge cake—with his favorite frosting. She invited all sorts of friends, people who had never met Jeremy before but were happy to join in the general fun. Some were even close to his age. He got lots of presents—simple things, nothing elaborate. They played games and stood around the piano singing old songs.

And then Elena did something that shook Adam's faith in her instincts after all. She asked for quiet and announced that Jeremy had practiced a piece of music he wanted to play for them, and especially for his father.

"Jeremy?" she said, motioning toward the piano. "Are you ready to play 'Musical Waves' for us?"

Adam looked quickly at his son. Jeremy's face was drained of all color. He looked nervously around the room, then met Adam's gaze. His eyes widened with panic and he turned and ran.

Adam grimaced. Hadn't she known this would happen?

"Sorry, everyone," he said. "Maybe next time."

Elena was beside him and she touched his arm. "Maybe this time," she whispered. "Go and talk to him, Adam. Have some faith in him."

He didn't want to do it. He'd had nothing but disappointment from trying to talk his son into things. But something in the determined set of her jaw convinced him. He would give it one more try.

He found Jeremy lying face down on his bed. As he sat down beside him he had no idea what he could say to make him come back and play his piece. But looking down at his tear-stained face, he remembered feeling the same way at times when he was a kid. Hesitantly, he reached out and tousled Jeremy's blond hair.

"Hey," he said. "I know how you feel. Some things are really hard to do."

Jeremy buried his face in his pillow.

Adam took a deep breath. "Listen. You like Elena, don't you?"

Jeremy looked up slowly and nodded, looking sullen.

"She's proud of the way you've learned to play the piano so quickly. She told everyone about it and she wanted to show you off. That's all."

Jeremy stared up at him, listening.

"We want Elena to be happy, don't we? More than anything."

Jeremy nodded.

"Good. I thought you would agree with me on that. So let's figure out a way we can make that happen. I've got an idea."

He was still looking up, so Adam had at least a glimmer of hope. Now to come up with an idea. He had to think fast and he could use a little luck.

And he got it. A few minutes later, after explaining the plan to the others, he was leading his son back to the piano and Lisa, the neighbor, was helping to herd the crowd out into the backyard. Jeremy sat down next to Elena on the piano bench and she drew him closer with an arm around his shoulders, whispered something in his ear, and then sat back and began to play the simple tune along with him. They played to an empty room, but, once Jeremy got going, one by one the others came creeping back in, each taking a seat in a semi-circle on the floor around the piano. Adam came in last and stayed in the back of the room. And as Jeremy gained confidence, Elena faded back until he was all alone, playing for the entire bunch. When it was over, he looked up as though he was surprised he'd actually done it, and everyone around the piano broke into cheers and applause. Elena hugged him. But he looked around until he found his father, and then he smiled.

Adam's heart swelled with pride and relief. And something else—a huge helping of paternal love. And when the party was over, Jeremy was tired but beaming.

"This was my best birthday ever," he murmured sleepily as his father carried him out to his bed.

"Well," Elena said when they were alone. "How did you think it went?"

He grabbed her around the waist and twirled her through the living room. "He smiled at me," he told her, ecstatic. "Elena! He smiled at me!"

She was delighted and laughing. "All this for one little smile?" she said.

"Are you kidding? He hasn't smiled at me like that since he was about four years old. This is a wonderful day."

And he kissed her.

It was a short kiss. A very quick kiss. A mere brushing of the lips. But she was dizzy from the spinning and the kiss only compounded the effect. He drew back right away and went on talking. But she was reeling and reaching out in her private darkness, wishing with all her heart she could see his eyes. She had to know what he was feeling and she wasn't getting enough from his voice. If only she knew...

Adam regretted the kiss even before he'd finished kissing her. He wasn't supposed to be confusing her this way. He'd promised himself to keep hands off and he meant to keep that promise. But he could see by her expression that he'd upset her.

"Elena," he began, taking her hands in his. But whatever he'd been about to say flew out of his mind when he saw that her eyes were brimming with tears. "What is it?" he said, alarmed. "Elena, have I done something…?"

"No." She half laughed, shaking her head. Reaching up, she put her hand against his cheek. "No, Adam. It's not you. It's me. There are times when it is just so hard…"

Her voice choked and she turned away, but he thought he knew what she was trying to say. "The blindness, you mean?" he asked softly.

She nodded, pressing her lips together. He pulled her into his arms. For just a moment, he held her. He could hardly breathe. She felt like heaven against him, her head resting on his chest, the scent of her hair filling his senses. It was agony when she pulled away, but he had to let her go. He knew what would happen if he didn't.

"You handle it so well," he said, catching hold of her hand so she couldn't get too far away. "But I'm sure there are times when it seems so unfair."

She nodded again, regaining control very quickly. "And I'm one of the lucky ones," she noted. "I do have memory of sight. Of course, over the years my memory has probably been contorted by my very active imagination. I probably see a much more colorful and unique world than you do."

She smiled, wiping her tears away, and his heart ached for her. "I don't know how you can be so calm about it," he said. "If it were me, I'd be railing at the heavens daily."

"I spent six months that way when I was about thirteen," she admitted. "All I did was cry. My poor mother." She shook her head, remembering. "But I came to realize that didn't do me any good. Trying to live a normal life does me a lot of good. So that's what I concentrate on."

He stared at her. "You've got so much to deal with," he said musingly, "and you've had it pretty hard. And yet, all you seem to do is think about how you can help other people." He touched her hair. It slipped through his fingers like gold coins. "Are you for real, lady?" he asked her softly.

She laughed, turning so that his fingers brushed her cheek before she drew away. "It's all selfish," she told him. "Making other people happy makes me happy. And I like to be happy." She sobered. "But, Adam, you're the one with the hard decisions to make right now. I only wish I could help you somehow."

He laughed softly, marveling at her. She was doing it again. You just couldn't stop the woman. He longed to take her in his arms again but he knew what that would lead to, so, reluctantly, he backed away.

Still, the entire episode just showed that, as usual, Elena was right. Which brought up Adam's main problem right now. From a personal point of view, he didn't know how he was going to get along without her. She'd become so important to him in such a short time, it was amazing.

She was totally focused on New York now. He'd been trying to help her get ready to go, and so had Gino. The two of them still tended to circle each other warily, but, he had to admit, Gino had done a good thing in contacting the school and letting them know about Elena's needs and special qualifications. If it hadn't been for him, all this wouldn't be happening.

The next day, while planning her packing, Elena was full of questions about New York. "What is it really like? Are the buildings really so tall? Are there really so many of them? Do the people all walk as fast as they say?" He tried to answer those, but then there were new ones. "Will I be able to find my way? Will it be too fast, too confusing? Will I...will I fail?"

He answered them all as honestly as he could, especially the last.

"No, you will not fail! You will, in fact, take New York by storm. Guaranteed, everyone in that school will know who you are by the end of the first month."

She still looked worried. "I'll have Fabio with me. Thank God for that."

"Yes. You'll do fine."

But actually, Adam was a little scared himself. How was she going to cope in that huge city? It would be so different from what she was used to.

"I suppose I'll be dating men," she said suddenly that evening as they sat at the table in the backyard and drank an after dinner coffee.

Caught in the middle of a sip, he sputtered and splashed coffee all over and had to wipe up the residue. "What?" he demanded as he mopped it up with a napkin. "What are you talking about?"

"I'm not a plaster saint, you know," she insisted, nose in the air.

She was getting tired of the way Adam treated her. She'd been thinking it over. If she let things drift the way they'd been all week, she was going to get nothing more than a handshake from this man at the airport. And in her new energetic state, that wasn't going to do.

She felt as though she was on a constant high lately. The excitement, the anticipation, the worry, the apprehension—it was almost too much to integrate all at once. This was all happening so quickly. She could hardly wait to go, and yet she dreaded it at the same time. How could she leave her beloved island?

"Every little bird has got to leave the nest and fly sometime," Gino told her over and over, until she wanted to scream—or at least tell him to find another saying to torture her with.

But it was true. And yet…how could she leave just when she'd met this man she was so very crazy about? He was…well, he was wonderful. Oh, she knew he had flaws. She could hear them. But who didn't? And she knew he was a man she could never have. So the sensible side of her nature told her, "This is exactly the right time to leave—before you get in too deep. When you leave there will be tears. Leave now and they won't have to be so bitter." And she knew that was true as well.

But there *would* be tears. Oh, yes. In just one short week she had grown accustomed to his voice—and she loved it. She could tell from one word or one exclamation what his mood was, whether he'd been frustrated or found a rainbow, whether he was worried or proud of something he'd accomplished. The nuances of tone and modulation in his voice made his mood an open book to her and she reacted accordingly. She'd never known a man she could read so well.

And yet there was one area where she was completely at sea as to his true feelings. How did he feel about her? She couldn't really tell. There were times when she had strong indications that he was attracted to her. And there was often a warmth in his voice when he spoke to her. But if all that was true—why didn't he ever so much as touch her?

"I'm going to New York and I'm going to meet new people and I'm going to date men," she said firmly.

Adam winced.

It had only been hours before that Tours had let him know in no uncertain terms that it was time to make a break away from Elena and he'd just been looking at her with different eyes, thinking, *What if…?* And now this!

"Wait a minute," he said, frowning fiercely. "Why the sudden interest in men?"

"Why not? Don't you think it's time?"

He muttered something unintelligible and she went on. "It won't be like it is here where I've been protected all my life and I know everyone and everyone is looking out for me. I have to make my own way in the world and that involves men. Maybe even…" She paused for dramatic effect, just to make sure he was listening. "Maybe even sex."

He choked. "Are you trying to make me crazy?" he demanded in a strangled voice.

"Why, what do you mean?" she asked, all innocence.

He swallowed hard before he could go on. "I…I don't want to think about you dating men."

She frowned at him. "That's because you don't think I can handle myself around strange men."

"No, that's not it. Believe me." He shook his head. "You certainly did okay when we met. Remember?"

"What did you think of me?" she asked eagerly. "How did I come across at the time?"

He looked down at her sweet face and wanted to kiss her so badly, he could hardly talk. "Like you thought I was something unclean that had washed in with the tide."

"Hmm. That's not too inviting." She frowned, biting her lip. "I'd better work on my approach to potential lovers, don't you think?"

"No." He shook his head vehemently. "You did just great. Treat all men like the enemy. That'll keep you safe."

She threw up her hands. "Safe, but loveless."

"Elena!" He was writhing in agony. He hated talking about this, hated thinking about this, wished she weren't thinking about it. It was torture to keep his hands off her, but a worse torture would be to think of someone else touching her.

"You don't need love," he said unconvincingly. "You need to study. Study hard and come back soon and we'll…" His voice trailed off because he knew he couldn't promise her anything.

"We'll do what, Mr About-to-be-king? I'll get to wave at you as you ride by in a limousine?"

He stared at her. He had no idea she'd thought things through that far. He wanted to say, "Hell, no! I'll have you over to the palace for dinner all the time and we'll talk and laugh and it will be like…like this." But he couldn't say that because he'd been told explicitly that such things were not going to be allowed.

Not allowed. The entire concept was strange. He'd always thought once you became King you got to do what you wanted. That didn't seem to be the case. He was going to be a conditional king. That meant he got to keep his crown only if a group of old men thought he deserved to. He was going to be on a short leash at all times. This whole gig was looking more and more problematic.

But he needed the money. Without the money, he was down a creek without a paddle. He'd come here with the iron-clad determination to get the money and he was going to do what it took to get that done. If he didn't get the funds by the end of the month, Ryder Productions would be no more. He couldn't let that happen.

"I just want you safe," he said, looking at her and aching to hold her.

"Maybe you should come along to New York to protect me," she answered softly.

He let his gaze skim over her silky dark hair, her smooth creamy skin, the hint of a sprinkling of freckles on her nose, and said in a heartfelt tone, "I wish I could."

They were both quiet for a moment, thinking that over. There was a sense of electricity between them that wasn't usually there, as though something was going to happen if someone didn't stop it. Adam was thinking he ought to get up and leave before it did. He didn't want to do anything to hurt her in any way. But pure magnetism was holding him here. He couldn't seem to pull himself away from her.

"In spite of everything, I've got to be prepared for new things, you know," she said at last. She turned her face toward him thoughtfully. "I probably could use some lessons."

He stiffened. "What kind of lessons?" he asked suspiciously.

"Oh, I don't know." She waved a hand in the air. "Maybe…on how to date strange men."

He shook his head dismissively. "I know nothing about dating men. I've always stuck to women, myself."

"I think you could teach me a lot," she said, ignoring his silly joke. "After all, you're the one who made me think these things."

He turned on her in shocked outrage. "What? You're going to blame this on me?"

"Of course." Her smile was very aware. "But you know what? You've opened my eyes—so to speak—to a lot of things. You've made me feel things I never felt before and think things I never thought before." She sighed happily. "And now I know. I want to date men."

"Oh, God," he groaned, his head in his hands. *"Mea culpa. Mea maxima culpa."*

"What was that?" she asked, not sure she understood his words, though she darn well understood the sentiment behind them. And she was prepared to use it to her advantage if she could.

"Nothing." He sighed, balancing back in the chair so that only the two back legs were on the ground. "It's just painful to know that now I have more than ever to atone for." He shook his head. "You were sweet and wholesome when I got here, and look at you now. I guess you'd have to say I've ruined you."

She laughed. "Don't be ridiculous. You merely awakened me to things I'd been sleepwalking through." She squared her shoulders. "So tell me, when I go on my first date and he tries to kiss me—"

"There you go. That's it!" He came back down to earth with a thud as the front legs of his chair hit the ground. "No more. I don't want to hear about any kissing." He finally had the motivation he needed to get him up out of his seat and start his retreat from the situation. "I'll teach you how to box," he said, rising from the table. "Much more useful." He picked up their cups and began to carry them back into the kitchen, hoping to change the subject by walking out on it.

She recoiled, then rose to follow him. She wasn't going to give this up. "What for?" she demanded.

"So you can defend yourself against lechers," he said back over his shoulder.

"But I don't want to defend myself," she cried after him. "I want to be kissed."

Adam put the dishes on the counter and turned to face her as she entered the kitchen behind him.

"Elena," he began, but she startled him by taking hold

of the front of his shirt and pulling him toward her, and whatever he'd been about to say evaporated into the ether.

"Are you going to show me how it's done?" she challenged him. "Or do I have to go out and beg kisses from men in the street?"

He looked down at the way she was arching toward him. She was so open, so lovely. He knew it would be so easy to take advantage of her sweet innocent vulnerability. He couldn't do that. Could he?

"Last chance," she whispered, presenting her full red lips to him like a gift. "Take it or leave it."

"Okay," he murmured back, his resistance crumbling as his body yearned for her. "Just a little one. Just…"

She gave his shirtfront a sharp tug and then his lips touched hers, and it was all over.

She'd known it would be this way. It was funny, but nothing about it surprised her. She'd known she would sink into his kiss and feel as if she were floating away. She'd known the kiss would start slowly and get harder. She'd known he would get caught up in it and not want to end it too soon. All that went according to plan.

But then she realized they were entering uncharted waters. She hadn't known his hands would feel so good sliding down her body. That the more of his kiss she got, the hungrier she would be for even more. That his raw desire would flare so quickly and take her breath away. And, most of all, she wasn't prepared for the urgency that curled through her blood and made her rub her breasts against his hard chest as though she had to have all he had to offer or die on the spot.

"Oh!" she cried, pulling back, astonished with herself.

He swore softly, shaking his head. "Elena, I'm sorry," he began.

"Sorry!" she cried. "Do you know how long I've been waiting for you to kiss me?"

He turned away. That wasn't what she'd hoped for and a sharp flash of disappointment made her feel sick to her stomach. Now she was embarrassed. He probably regretted the whole thing. She could feel the tension in him, feel how hard he had to work to keep an even keel. She'd thrown him off his carefully maintained casual calm and he didn't like that.

She wasn't sure why he was always so particular with her. Was it just because she was blind? Did he treat her as though she were made of porcelain because her disability scared him? Was he afraid of hurting her somehow?

Or was he afraid to get entangled with someone he knew he could have no future with? Or was she just plain wrong about him? Maybe she just wasn't his type.

But that couldn't be it. Not entirely. She'd felt his body respond to her more than once. Nothing in her life had ever been more exciting. Why did he keep trying to deny it?

Whatever the reason was, she knew she'd done something that had upset him and she was sorry about that. But she couldn't regret the kiss. No. That was a memory she would cherish for the rest of her life.

She heard him go off toward the guest house and she sank into a chair and closed her eyes. Very soon she would be gone. But how long would it take to leave regrets behind?

* * *

Adam was at the palace the next afternoon sitting across the desk from three of the king's counselors, including Tours, and finding it very difficult to stay friendly with them. He had just finished reading the actual list of rules set up for the lucky person who won the job as King, a long list of ten items, most of which annoyed him like crazy. That was bad enough.

But then came the set of conditions put together just for him. He was to break it off with Elena. Jeremy was to be sent off to boarding school in Switzerland. And he was to make sure his mother never set foot on the island, not even for his coronation. The funny thing was, just a week ago, sending Jeremy off to boarding school wouldn't have seemed so impossible. Now that he had transformed himself into a normal child, things were different.

"It looks to me like the king has less freedom than any of his subjects," he commented, having difficulty remaining civil.

"Of course. That's the way it always is. Didn't you know that?"

No, he hadn't known it. And he didn't like it, either.

But he was having a hard time focusing on rules right now. His mind was still stuck on kissing Elena and he couldn't seem to get it to move on.

Kissing her had not been a good idea. He'd known it wouldn't be. That was why he'd avoided doing it all this time. Once he'd kissed her, he knew it was only going to be that much harder to pretend he could walk away from her at the end of the week. That he could watch her take off for New York and wave goodbye and go on with his life. Wasn't going to happen. He was still going to have to walk away and she was still going to take off in a silver plane. But now it was going to hurt like hell.

Of course, it would have hurt anyway. But now he had a reason to let it hurt even more. He was all tangled in regrets and wishes and pure, hot, unabated desire for her golden body, and they were coming at him with these pointless rules? His anger was starting to build. If he didn't watch out, he was going to do something stupid, something that would ruin his chances of getting the money. The money that he had to have. The money that was at the root of all this misery.

He looked Tours straight in the eye and didn't hedge. "How about the money?" he asked. "How soon can I get a portion of my allotment?"

"I can have it entered into your account right away," Tours replied, naming an amount that made Adam blink. "As soon as you sign the contract."

The contract. He could sign it right now and get the money to Zeb by tomorrow. His company would be saved. Production could get back on track for two major films that were idling, waiting for funds. The sun would break through the clouds and everything would be coming up roses.

That was one side of the coin. The other wasn't so happy. Jeremy would be heading for boarding school. He would have to tell his mother she wasn't allowed to come to his coronation. And, worst of all, Elena would be out of his life for ever.

Tours put the contract on the table and put a pen

alongside it. The three men sat and stared at him. He stared at the contract. It was "do or die" time.

But then, it wasn't, because at that moment his cell phone rang. Glancing at the screen, he could see that it was probably Elena.

He popped it open. "Hi," he said. "What is it?"

"It's…oh, Adam, it's Jeremy!"

Elena sounded frantic.

He sat up straighter. "What about Jeremy?"

"He's gone."

"What are you talking about?"

"It's been hours now. I didn't want to call you there at the palace, but we've looked everywhere and we can't find them."

His heart was thumping with apprehension. "Elena, start at the beginning. What's happened?"

"Jeremy and Fabio are missing. I think he's taken Fabio and run away."

"Why would he do that?"

"Oh, Adam! He overheard some things. Gino was telling me that the rumor is that the palace is going to insist you send Jeremy off to boarding school and he heard that and got very worried. So I sat him down and tried to explain everything. I don't think he'd understood until now exactly what was happening, how you were going to be King and how I was going to New York and taking Fabio with me. And I guess I made a mess of it. He was very upset."

Adam closed his eyes and groaned. This wasn't Elena's fault. It was his own. He'd been putting off explaining everything to Jeremy. He should have done so from the beginning. Who better than he to try to get it right?

Because deep down he knew just how Jeremy felt. The boy saw people he depended on fading from his life. He felt betrayed and deserted by those he loved the most. He was afraid he was about to lose everyone he cared about. Yes, Adam understood those feelings. He'd been there often enough himself. Hell, he was always there.

"I let him take Fabio and go off to play for awhile. I thought that might calm him down. And now they're gone."

"I'll be right there," he said and flipped the phone closed. "I've got to go," he told Tours, rising from his chair.

"That will be impossible," the stuffy man intoned importantly. "The contract must be signed. And we've scheduled a meeting with King Giorgio at exactly three o'clock. The meeting is mandatory. There can be no postponement."

Adam closed his eyes for just a moment. This was what he'd been waiting for—a meeting with his grandfather. His entire future might hang in the balance. He hesitated only a few seconds, his fate flashing before his eyes, then briskly shook his head.

"I'll be back when I can," he told Tours. "I'll sign your damn contract. But my son is in trouble. And my son comes first."

Turning on his heel, he left the room, despite the shout that followed him down the hall. King Giorgio would have to wait. Jeremy was more important.

CHAPTER NINE

ADAM knew that nothing was more guaranteed to put your heart in your throat than searching for a missing child. Every horrible thing that could possibly happen to Jeremy suddenly seemed like a looming probability, from falling down a well to being kidnapped by terrorists. Adam had to settle himself and block such things from his mind in order to think. If he were Jeremy, and his heart had been broken, where would he go?

It had to be somewhere not too far away. And it had to be a place where dogs could go, too. His mind leaped to the most probable place. The Roman ruins, where they had all first found each other.

Leaving Elena behind with Gino, he raced to the ruins. It was a cool, windy day and only a few tourists straggled about on the remnants of the villa. He climbed the wall and looked down on the patio where he'd first seen Elena, but there wasn't a sign of Jeremy.

"Jeremy!"

He tried calling every few minutes as he scrambled along the ledge, then down along the shore. The cliffs stretched out to the bend and beyond and he wondered how many caves they hid. The ruins lay behind him now. Instinct drove him on and he ran along the shore, scanning above for any sign of life.

He'd almost given up when he heard a dog's bark. Freezing, he listened hard. There it was again. Hope flashed through him. He called Jeremy's name and there was the dog again, and this time he could locate him, high along a rocky crag, peering over the edge. Forgetting how tired he was, he began climbing quickly, heading for Fabio. His shoes weren't made for climbing and he slipped back a yard for every two he gained, but he made steady progress.

The ledge where Fabio stood, wagging his tail and barking, was inaccessible from below. He had to climb around and get into position where he could look down. The whole time he'd been afraid to let himself wonder why Jeremy wasn't looking over the edge with the dog. And once he got into place, he knew. Jeremy was lying on the rocks. He'd obviously fallen from above. His face was bloody and his arm was twisted in a strange way beneath him. Adam's heart sank.

"Jeremy!"

He'd cut his hands on the rocks but he didn't notice. After a quick call for help on his cell phone, he began the slow, painful climb down to where Jeremy was. He slipped. He fell. He cut himself and bruised himself. But finally, he made it.

"Jeremy!" He went right to his boy and touched his

neck, finding a pulse. "Thank God!" He worked carefully, Fabio watching over them both, to free Jeremy's broken arm.

"Ow," Jeremy murmured, then opened his huge blue eyes.

"Dad?" he said weakly. "Dad! I was scared you were going to send me away."

Adam cupped his son's face with his hands. "Jeremy, don't you know yet that I'll never send you away? Never. Where I go, you go. And that's a promise."

Jeremy sighed. His eyes closed, and he was out like a light.

Adam closed his own eyes, but only to say a short prayer of gratitude. As the rescue workers appeared on the cliff above them he let his relief flood in and fill his heart. His boy was going to be okay. He wasn't going to let it go any other way.

The halls of the hospital echoed as Elena walked down them, letting Fabio lead her. She knew he would find them without having to be told where to go. And he did.

They went into a room and she put a hand on Adam's shoulder, startling him out of a fitful doze.

"Hi," he said, rising out of the chair and getting another one for her. "Sit down. He's still out of it."

"How does he look?" she asked worriedly. "Is his face bad?"

"Not really. He had to have some stitches on the cut across his forehead. It'll probably leave a great scar."

"A great scar!" she scoffed. "Men."

He grinned, rubbing his unshaven face. "All in all, he'll be okay."

She nodded. "What was the final inventory on his injuries?"

"Broken humerus, broken collar bone, two cracked ribs, cuts and bruises. And a concussion."

"Wow. That's a lot for a young boy."

"Young bones heal fast."

"Do you know exactly what happened?"

"No. He'll tell us when he can."

"Of course."

She sat quietly for a moment. She couldn't see him but she was pretty sure she knew what she would see if she could—a very tired man. She could hear his exhaustion in his voice.

"You really should go home and get some sleep," she said, though she knew very well how he would answer that.

"Not until he wakes up," Adam said, stretching. "I have to be here when he wakes up."

She nodded, settling back into the chair next to him. "Me, too," she said stoutly.

Looking over at her, he smiled with undisguised affection. "You don't need to do this."

"Yes, I do. I love Jeremy, too. And he cares about me, and Fabio. So let him see all the people who care about him here when he wakes up."

"Okay," Adam said softly. "You win."

"Always," she reminded him, but her smile was melancholy, knowing what an empty boast that was.

Suddenly, his hand was there, reaching out for hers. She took hold of his and held very tightly, as though they were forming a lifeline. She wished she would never have to let go.

"I was just about to sign the contract," he said suddenly. "When you called. I had the pen in my hand."

"Why didn't you go ahead and sign it?"

He shook his head. "I could have, I suppose. But once I heard Jeremy was missing, that was all I could think about."

She nodded. They sat in silence for a long time, and finally, she said, "Don't sign it."

He looked at her, startled. "What do you mean?"

"Don't sign it. Don't become King. Oh, Adam…"

He pulled his hand away from hers. "Does this mean you still think I don't deserve the crown?"

"Not at all." She turned toward him, wishing she knew how to explain. "It means you deserve better. Oh, Adam, there has to be another way. If you really don't have any other way of getting the money…"

"That's not an option. Don't you think I exhausted every resource I could think of before agreeing to come here to Niroli? Taking the crown was my bottom line last chance."

She bit her lip and thought for a bit longer. "Let it go," she said softly at last. "Adam, just let it go."

"Ryder Productions?"

She nodded.

"That's crazy. Ryder Productions is my life. That's like telling me to let my life go."

"You can start again. Start fresh. Start a new company."

His laugh was utterly humorless. "I guess I never told you about the fifteen months when I lived on macaroni and cheese while I was trying to put my company together, did I? I spent two months living in my car. I drained my bank and credit accounts and the bank and credit accounts of everyone I could persuade to believe in me along the way. And for awhile I thought I was going to have to face all those people with the bad news that I'd squandered all their money for nothing." He shook his head. "I can't go through that again. You have to be twenty-one and stupid to do those things. It's too late to start again."

She groped for his hand and, when she found it, she held it tightly. "Adam, think about this. What if it just isn't meant to be. What if you are doing this for all the wrong reasons."

He laced his fingers with hers. "Such as?"

She took a deep breath. "Well, maybe you're here trying to take the crown because you want revenge on the royal family for what they did to you and your mother. Oh, not consciously, I know. But deep down, on another level. Is that possible? Think it over, Adam."

"Revenge," he scoffed. "What good would revenge do for me?"

"That's exactly the point. From what you've told me, life here as King would be hell on earth for you. The council would force you to do things you would hate. You would never be free to live as you want to, to do what you want to." *To love whom you want to,* she could have added, but didn't quite dare. "Adam, despite what you've said, you are not your company. And more than that, you're not just a boss and a production guy and a business manager. You are a father and a friend and a wonderful person in your own right. You are your own man. You have value. And you're worth more than your company ever could be worth."

He shook his head. "Elena, that's just crazy," he said, but his voice didn't quite carry the conviction it had a few minutes earlier. He had to admit she had brought up some points he hadn't considered. He was so focused on saving his company. Maybe he ought to focus a little more on saving his life.

They sat in silence for two more hours, both thinking about what she'd said. Time crept by. They took turns drifting off to sleep for a few minutes at a time. But their hands didn't lose the bond. And they were still holding on when Jeremy finally woke.

"Look," Adam said pointlessly. "He's moving."

She jumped up along with him and Fabio joined them at the bedside.

"Dad!"

It was the first thing he said and Adam's heart swelled. Jeremy blinked groggily. Adam reached in and tousled his hair.

"Hey, kid," he said. "How you feeling?"

"Okay." His eyes widened as he noticed the others. "Elena. Fabio!"

"Hello, darling," Elena said, touching his face lightly. "I'm so glad you're awake."

He grabbed her hand and held it. "Elena, I was really afraid you would be gone already."

"I wouldn't go without saying goodbye to you, sweetie. I'm not leaving until Monday."

He pressed her hand to his heart and said tearfully, "I wish you didn't have to go."

"But I want to go. I need to go." She smiled at him. "What I wish is that I could take you with me."

He nodded and his eyes began to drift shut again. They drew back, letting him rest. But Adam pulled Elena into his arms and dropped a quick kiss on her lips.

"Thank you for being here," he murmured close to her ear. "I don't know what I'm going to do without you."

She felt tears stinging her eyes and, when he released her, she turned away. She didn't know, either. Right now, she was completely confused about everything. Except for one thing. She knew she loved Adam Ryder, the future King of Niroli. That was the one certainty in her life.

A good night's sleep left Adam feeling refreshed, but not revived. There were too many uncertainties about his life right now to let him be at peace in any way. But at least Jeremy was healing nicely. He was scheduled to be released in another day, and it didn't look as though there would be any lasting problems. And that was the most important thing, after all.

He made his way into the kitchen to see if breakfast was a possibility. The clock said almost noon, but time was hardly meaningful at the moment. He knew he would have to get to the palace and see what was going on there, but that could wait for an hour or so.

He was just pulling a carton of eggs out of the refrig-. erator when Elena came breezing in.

"Good morning, sleepy head," she said. "How are you feeling?"

"Fine. Great." He turned to smile at her, enjoying the way she brightened up a room. Then the light dimmed as he remembered. She would be gone in less than twenty-four hours. "Are you all packed and ready to go?"

"Just about. I've got my bags crammed with every-thing I could get into them. I've notified the various agencies who need to know I'll be gone. Gino is going to keep an eye on the house for me. My piano students have been loaned out to other teachers." She paused, head to the side.

"There's only one thing left on my agenda," she told him lightly. "Just one very important thing I want to get done before I leave."

He stepped back in surprise as she reached out for him, but the granite counter didn't give him much room to maneuver and her fingers unerringly found what they were looking for and began to work on his shirt, releas-ing one button after another.

"Hey," he said in alarm. "What are you doing?"

She gave him a secret smile. "Seducing you." His shirt was open and she flattened her hands on the hard muscles of his chest, catching her breath as she gathered in the masculine power he held there. "Oh!"

"What are you talking about?" he said, sounding desperate. He grabbed her hands to make her stop. "Elena… "

"You see," she went on, "I would have thought that *you* might want to seduce *me*. But I've been waiting all week and…nothing! There's not much time left. So I decided to take the situation into my own hands. So to speak."

His grip on her had loosened as though he was giving up, and she spread her hands out again, trying to catch every bit of him.

But he was shaking his head in consternation. "Elena, I can't…"

"Oh, yes, you can." She closed her eyes for a moment, savoring the feel of him, and when she spoke again her voice was husky with awareness.

"Remember when you made me go on the water slide? I was very scared and you promised you wouldn't let go of me. That made me brave enough to try it." Leaning forward, she rubbed her cheek against his chest, then pressed her lips there for just a few seconds. "Well, now it's my turn," she murmured. "I won't let go, either. You can trust me."

Adam knew he should be fighting her off, but he also knew he didn't have the moral strength to do it. And the way she was pretending she was the experienced one, taking him by the hand, was as adorable as it was unbelievable. Instead of pushing her away, he pulled her close and laughed low in his throat.

"Elena, are you sure…?"

"Oh, yes. I'm sure." She pulled her head back and turned her face up toward his. "I guess you can tell I've never done this before," she said, feeling a little shy all of a sudden. "I may never do it again. But I want this to be with you, Adam. Only you."

His groan came from deep within, a place that was dark and unhappy. "Elena, you deserve so much more."

"Really?" Her smile was radiant. "I'll tell you what I deserve. I deserve a man. A real man. A man with passion. And right now, in this moment, I deserve you."

The last remaining shreds of his resistance crumbled. But he'd known all along it was going to happen. It had to happen. His mouth covered hers and her arms came up to curl around his neck, letting her arch her warm body into his, and he gathered her in and held her so that as much of her was against him as possible. And he kissed her, kissed her softly, gently, almost reverently, tasting her sweetness, rasping his tongue against hers until she was yearning toward him, begging for more. And then he deepened the kiss, unleashing a hint of the hunger he had been keeping under control all this time. Now his kiss was harder, more demanding, getting greedy and drunk with the taste of her.

"Come with me." Taking his hand, she began to lead him into her bedroom.

She closed the bedroom door and turned to face him.

"Okay?" she asked, suddenly not as sure of herself.

"Okay," he murmured back, his hands already framing her face, his body already leaning into hers. Her small hands slipped his shirt from his shoulders and touched him lightly, here, there, everywhere, exploring and testing. He groaned with pleasure, then began to work on removing her sweater, his fingers trembling with anticipation.

Her full, pink-tipped breasts were so beautiful, his heart nearly stopped when she released them.

"Oh, Elena," he whispered, touching the tips with his fingers and watching them tighten into high, hard buds. "Oh, my God. If only you could see how beautiful you are."

She felt beautiful and that was all that mattered at the moment. By now they were both naked and on her lace-covered bed. She stretched and purred under his wonderful hands, but she needed his mouth again and she found it, opening her lips and coaxing him back where he belonged.

She felt it all, just as she knew she had to. She felt how his heart sped up, how his muscles hardened, how his skin dampened, how his tongue became a weapon of plunder in her mouth. And very soon his skin was sizzling with life, burning with desire.

But his hands moved on her body, trailing lines of fire, drawing out her senses, making her feel things she'd never felt before. As they cupped her breasts, rubbing ecstasy against her nipples, she felt passion begin to smolder between her legs and her body began to move of its own volition.

Oh, please, please, she thought deliriously. *I've waited so long.*

But aloud she only moaned and moved.

Adam had gone over the edge by now. He was in a state of white-hot desire. He'd thought he would have no trouble keeping control. After all, he wasn't inexperienced, not as she was. He'd done this before.

Or had he? Maybe not. This was different. There was something about her that seemed to heighten each sensation, add a touch of excitement to each move, sweeten each moment. And now he felt himself lose all moorings and become nothing but a man overwhelmed with the deep, hungry need for one special woman.

He stroked her, preparing her, trying to be as gentle as he could, but his urgency was taking over and he had to have her now.

"Elena?" he rasped out.

"Oh, please," she cried. "Now, Adam! Please."

He entered as carefully as he could manage, knowing he would probably hurt her, but she didn't seem to notice that. Her urgency was as frenzied as his and she clung to him, urging him on, crying out as the pulse between them became a passionate dance. Her hips rose higher and higher, driving him harder and deeper, until she thought she would die.

But she didn't. As things slowed and the sensation began to fade, she relaxed, letting her cramped fingers open, catching her breath. But the pulse took a long time to taper away. She ached, but the sense of satisfaction and fulfillment was so much stronger than the pain. And the world was full of rejoicing.

"Ah," she said, reaching for where he lay beside her. "Listen. Music."

"Music?" He raised his head and listened. "I don't hear any music."

There, you see, she said sadly, though only to herself, *you're not in love.*

But she was. This was all she would ever have of the man she had fallen so deeply in love with. It wasn't enough. She would spend the rest of her life regretting that she couldn't find a way to keep him.

But it was better to have had this moment, this closeness, with such a man than to have it all with someone she didn't love this way.

"Adam?"

"Yes?"

She turned to face him, letting her hand trail over his deliciously cooling skin.

"Kiss me again."

"Any time."

And she sighed with pleasure as he kept his word.

CHAPTER TEN

ADAM was late for his meeting at the palace. The faces that met him there were not friendly. In fact, they were becoming downright hostile. Here he was, ready to sign the contract, and they were acting as if they were having second thoughts. After a short lecture on keeping appointments and how important that would be in his future life as a royal, they had a new tack with him.

"We have a lady here we'd like you to talk to. She's an award-winning historian who specializes in Nirolian history. We think talking to her will help ground you in the background of this country and the place you could play in it."

"Fine," Adam said. Anything was better than these deadly dull meetings. "When can she meet with me?"

"She's here right now, in the library. Tours will escort you."

It wasn't until he was walking down the marble halls to the library that it occurred to him the historian might be Elena's friend. And sure enough, when Tours opened

the huge double doors to allow him to enter, there stood
Susan Nablus.

"Adam!" she said, coming forward to greet him.
"Such a pleasure. Please sit down. I hear you need a
little micro-history of Nirolia."

He was about to protest that he needed no such thing,
that Elena had made sure he knew as much as he would
ever need, but there was a significant look in her eye that
stopped him. And then she gave him a surreptitious
wink. That sealed his lips until Tours was gone.

"Oh, I know, I know," she said, shaking her head as
he began to protest that he didn't need a history lesson.
"But when they said they wanted you to meet with me,
I thought it a fine opportunity to show you something
important I found in your father's papers. I've begun
work in the archives here in the castle, and one of the
first things I found was a letter addressed to you."

Adam went very still. He didn't say a word, just
waited. But there was a buzzing in his ears and for a
moment he thought maybe this was the way people felt
just before they fainted.

"Unfortunately, I can't let you have it," she was
saying. "But I thought you ought to read it. Here it is."

She took a paper out of a long folder and slid it across
the desk to him. Slowly, very slowly, he reached for it.
And he began to read.

This letter is to the son I never knew. I saw you
last week in Rome. We came face to face and
when I saw the look in your eyes, I knew who you

were right away. I couldn't acknowledge you then. And I can't acknowledge you publicly now. But I do want to put into words what I would have liked to have said to you there in the department store. So I will do so here and hope that, some day, you will read this.

Adam read it very quickly, skimming and rushing, needing to swallow it all in one big gulp. And then he went back over it, savoring certain passages, smiling at others, frowning when something struck him wrong. And then again, a third time. And he was through.

Looking up at Susan, he smiled and slid the letter back across the desk. "Thank you," he said simply. "You've given me a precious gift. I finally feel as though I once had a living, breathing father. That's a feeling I've never had before."

"I'm glad," she said softly.

There were tears in her eyes, and for a moment he wondered why, and then he realized he had tears on his face. Laughing, he wiped them away. Real tears. A real father.

He told Elena about it that night while they were sitting in the dark garden, looking up at the moon.

"So, what did your father have to say?" she asked curiously.

"Not much, actually. Just that he was sorry he hadn't been around for me when I needed him. That he wished he knew me. That he wished I knew my brothers and sisters. I suppose I'll be meeting them one of these days."

"And that was enough to send you back walking on air?"

He grinned. "Yes, damn it! That was enough. I have a father who knew I existed. That's more than I had yesterday. It's not enough, of course, in the greater scheme of things, but it's something."

Elena nodded thoughtfully. "You see how important your father is to you? Even a father you only know on paper?"

"And your point is?"

"Think of Jeremy and what he needs from you. Don't let your life as royalty rob you of a son the way it did your father."

She was right and he knew it. He was going to keep Jeremy with him no matter what. If the Niroli crown was taken away from him because he refused to send his son away, then maybe it wasn't worth it. That was the way it was going to have to be. Tomorrow he would sign the contract at last. But he would strike out the rule about his son. And if that brought about a major crisis, so be it.

Moving closer, she snuggled against his shoulder. "I'm going to miss these evenings together," she said softly.

"Me, too," he responded, burying his face in her soft, fragrant hair. "How am I going to make it through my days without you telling me what to do every night?"

Laughing, she pulled back and pretended to hit him in the arm. He caught her largely ineffective fist and brought it to his lips, peeling back the fingers and kissing the palm.

"Ooh," she whispered. "That feels very sexy."

"Good," he whispered back. "Because I feel very sexy, too."

She lifted her face to him and he kissed her. This time they would go slow and take things easy, he promised himself. And then she parted her lips and invited him in and his blood began to race and he knew his plans were out the window again.

Later that night he slept while Elena lay beside him, tears sliding down her face and dampening her pillow. To have found paradise and then be forced to walk away—this was the sort of pain she'd never experienced before. Adam Ryder was the man she loved. She would never love another man the way she loved him.

So she was grateful for this time with him, but agonized over leaving him. She even had fleeting thoughts of canceling her flight and staying. But she knew that would be useless. In a matter of days, he would walk away and never look back. And then where would she be? No lover, and no career, either. Try as she might, she couldn't figure a way out of that one.

So she would take a silver plane to another continent, and he would take a golden crown into another world.

"'And never the twain shall meet'," she whispered to herself, and the tears came again.

The time had come. Elena didn't want a big send-off at the airport, so she hadn't told anyone the details of her flight. Just Gino. All her goodbyes had been said the night before. Gino would handle the final departure.

But she hadn't counted on how sad it was going to feel.

"No crying," Gino warned her after he took a look at the tragedy in her face. "I don't do crying."

"I'm not going to cry," she reassured him hopefully. If she kept her mind off Adam, she might actually be able to keep her promise. "I may whimper, but I would never cry."

"You don't blame me, do you?" he asked her.

She turned toward him in surprise. "For what?"

"For getting the school to contact you. For making you go to New York, just when you were falling in love with Adam Ryder."

She turned away. "Who says I'm falling in love with Adam?" she asked, but somehow her bravado didn't sound convincing.

"It's only obvious. Now whether the guy himself knows it is another story. He seems to be thick as a brick."

She laughed. If there was anything Adam wasn't...

But there was no more time to talk.

"They're calling for my flight," she said. "Give me a hug. And thank you for being my fairy godmother."

"I'm not sure I like that designation," he said, though he did laugh. "Goodbye, sweetheart. Go out there and grab what you want out of life. You deserve the best."

He hugged her, gave Fabio a last scratch behind the ears, and they were off, walking down the ramp to the holding area, and Elena's heart started to pound. This was it. She was cutting her ties to her past and she was going to be on her own. Would she sink or swim? Only time would tell.

A half-hour later, she was in her seat on the plane. Luckily, they weren't fully booked and there was room on the floor next to her in the bulkhead seat for Fabio to stretch out. The flight attendant had stopped by to make sure she was comfortable and to offer any assistance she might need.

"Just speak up," she said. "Don't be shy. We're here to help you. It's our job."

Her friendly attitude helped make Elena feel a bit easier about the flight. She had flown before. She'd taken trips to Europe as a young girl. But she'd been with her grandmother. This time, she was all alone.

"Except you for, Fabio," she murmured, touching the dog's proud head.

She had the middle seat in a bank of three and there was no one on either side, so she could lean back and think about the last few days and how Adam Ryder had changed her life. Eventually, she hoped she could think about him and not have tears fill her eyes. But for now the tears were a constant, and, despite her excitement at going to New York, she was heartsick.

At least she was striking out on her own. At least she was following her star. At least she was doing all those other trite and hackneyed things she'd once thought were the most important things in the world to her. Now she knew better. Love and people who cared about you—that was what mattered. And that was what she was losing right now.

It seemed they were closing the doors and preparing for take-off. Elena sat back and tried to relax. There was some sort of commotion a few rows behind her. She tried to listen hard to see what it might be, but she couldn't filter the many voices out and interpret what was going on. And then the voices died down and the sounds were again of getting ready for take-off.

And then…another sound. Fabio's tail was thumping on the floor of the cabin.

"Fabio?" she said questioningly. "What on earth…?"

"He's just saying hello," said a familiar voice from just behind her seat. "Which, I notice, you're not doing."

"Adam?"

She shook her head. Was she dreaming? Sometimes, when you wanted something so badly you thought you might actually die if you didn't get it, your mind played tricks on you. Was that what this was? She groped for sanity. "Adam, is that you?"

"Yes, Elena," he said, sliding into the seat beside her. "It's me."

"But what…? How…?"

"And it's me, too," Jeremy said, levering himself into the seat on the other side of her, his crutches already second nature to him. He reached out to touch her cheek with his little-boy hand. "Hi. I just got out of the hospital. They put a needle in my arm, but I didn't cry. And then they gave me popsicles to eat. They said popsicles were good for me, to keep from getting a fever or something. So…"

"Okay, Jeremy," Adam said, motioning for him to get down into his seat. "The seat-belt light is on. Better stay put until we get up into the air."

Elena was still in a daze. Just having them with her

was joyful, but she still didn't understand how it had happened. "What are you two doing here?"

"We decided to go to New York," Adam told her. "Everybody's doing it. It seems like the place to be. I might even start a new production company there."

"A new company?" She was so out to sea. "What happened to your old company?"

"I'm afraid that's over. Oh, and the king thing is over, too. I decided against it."

Jeremy was talking a mile a minute and she couldn't even process what Adam was saying, not to mention both of them talking at once. She held up a hand in each direction. "Stop and start at the beginning. You!" She pointed at Adam. "Now tell me what happened."

"I'll tell you what happened. I went in to the palace to sign the contract. I was ready to do it. I actually felt I had no choice. I had to try to save my company."

She nodded. She knew all that. "And?"

"I looked down at the paper and realized they wanted me to sign away the two people I love most in the world. And I sat there with the pen in my hand and realized I couldn't do it."

She shook her head. "You mean Jeremy and your mother?"

He leaned closer. "I mean Jeremy and you."

"Me?" She squeaked it out and didn't even feel chagrined. There was still too much to get into her head. She had no time to waste on being embarrassed.

"Hmm." Adam pretended to be thinking it over. "Is your name Elena Valerio?"

"Yes!"

"Then you're the one."

She turned toward him and suddenly he was kissing her. She loved that, but she still wanted to know…was this for real?

"Absolutely," Adam insisted, drawing back. "All the things we'd talked about were swirling in my head. I'd been able to stand back a little over the last few days and get a more realistic perspective on things. I realized I had to get my priorities in order. And once I did that, the way was clear."

"Oh, Adam, I'm so glad!"

"I left the palace and went to the hospital to get Jeremy and we dashed to the airport to see if we could catch the plane you were leaving on. That last run through the concourse was pretty wild. But we made it."

"We saw Gino," Jeremy told her. "He yelled something but we had to keep running."

She smiled at him and tousled his hair. "I'm glad you did," she said lovingly. "Are you planning to head straight for California? Or can you stay in New York for awhile?"

There was a moment of silence and she waited, heart beating, for her answer.

"Elena," Adam said at last. "I don't think you get it. We're going with you. And we're staying with you. We're in this brand-new life thing together."

Her heart skipped a beat. "You're not going back to Hollywood?"

"Nope. We're going to explore our possibilities in the big city. We'll see what the climate is for film production. I built one production company up from scratch. I can do it again."

"Oh, that's so…so…"

"'Wonderful' may be the word you're looking for. As in Wonderful Adam Ryder. It's a common way of referring to me."

"Right." She laughed. Happiness was shimmering through her. In her wildest dreams she could never have imagined that this could happen.

"I've already got this great idea for a film," he was saying, sounding pretty darn happy himself. "It could be a documentary about musical therapy and how it can help people. The story can be told through the experiences of a therapy student who arrives on the mean streets of New York with hope in her heart and a need to share her joy through music. Starring a gorgeous blind chick named Elena Valerio."

She tried to hide her smile but couldn't hold it back. "Cool," she said.

"Won't it be Elena Ryder?" Jeremy asked, looking worried

"What?" Elena's jaw dropped.

"Uh, look, Jeremy, I haven't asked her yet. You're not supposed to bring it up until I've actually asked her."

"Oh. Sorry." Jeremy snuggled close against her arm. "But you will marry us, won't you? Huh? Come on, Elena. Say yes."

"I'll take over, son," Adam said. "Though I do think you've done a masterful job so far." He leaned close to Elena's ear. "Chip off the old block, wouldn't you say?"

She laughed. Everything was striking her as funny now. "No doubt about it."

"Here's the deal, Elena." His voice deepened and he leaned so close, she could feel his breath on her face. "I love you. I know it's crazy. But I can't help it. So this is my plea. Please, please, please…marry me."

"Marry *us*," Jeremy muttered again stubbornly.

And Elena knew what her answer would be. She laughed through her tears. "The gorgeous blind chick says yes."

EPILOGUE

"DAD! It's snowing!"

Adam looked up from the full-length mirror where he was swearing over the impossibility of getting his cravat on straight. "You're supposed to be getting dressed," he reminded his son. "The wedding is in less than an hour."

Jeremy blinked at him happily. "I know but…it's snowing outside!"

"You've seen snow before. We went skiing at Aspen last winter and—"

"Dad, Elena has never been in the snow before. She told me."

Adam paused. "Really?"

The boy nodded eagerly. "She's gonna love it. We gotta take her out in it. Let's get her. Hurry."

Adam smiled, enjoying his son's enthusiasm. In the weeks since they'd left Niroli and settled in New York, he'd become a different person, open and loving and full of life. It was Elena's doing. Everything good in his life was Elena's doing. And today, he was going to marry her.

They were in separate rooms in the Moss Garden Wedding Chapel, preparing to make their bond official. Various friends were gathering in the sanctuary, some who had flown in from Niroli, others they had met since arriving in New York, mostly at the music school where Elena was studying. In the short time they had been here, they had already begun to build a new life together. Jeremy was enrolled in a good school. Adam's ideas for his new production company were attracting interest from some financial backers. The future was looking bright.

"Come on!" his son urged, tugging at his hand.

"We can't, Jeremy. I'm not supposed to see her before the ceremony. It's bad luck."

Jeremy frowned. "I thought you told me people make their own luck," he said impatiently. "Come on," he added, rushing to the window. "Just come and look how big the snowflakes are."

He followed the boy to the window and, to his surprise, the flakes were indeed unusually large. They hung in the late afternoon light like ornaments on a tree, glistening with a sense of magic. The patterns were plain to the naked eye. He'd never seen snow like this before—a special sense of enchantment for a very special day. Staring at them, he realized Jeremy was right. Elena had to experience this. And who knew how long it would last?

"Okay," he said, lurching into action. "We've got to get her fast. You go down the back stairs and wait. I'll go to the room where she is. You whistle if someone starts coming up. Okay?"

"Okay." Jeremy nodded happily, his eyes dancing with excitement. "Let's go."

Adam raced up the stairs and stopped at the door to the bridal chamber. The room was full of people. He should have known it would be. Opening the door a crack, he saw Gino and Natalia and a couple of other women he didn't know well all looking very intent on their bridesmaid chores. Only Fabio saw him and started to wag his tail. Even with the dog on his side, there was no way this bunch was going to let him come in and whisk away the bride. What now?

He went back onto the landing, trying to think of some sort of diversion he could create that would make them all scatter, but everything he thought of would get him in so much trouble, he might spend the night in jail rather than in his marriage bed. And he wasn't going to risk that.

Hearing footsteps, he turned and found Natalia had come out to see what he wanted.

"I saw you looking in, you naughty boy," she teased, though she had a watchful look in her eye. "You know that's against the rules."

"Natalia," he said, going to her and taking her hands in his. "It's snowing. I have to show Elena."

"Now?"

"Right now."

Natalia frowned. "Uh, I hate to remind you of this, but, you know, the lady is blind."

He smiled at her, a big, all-encompassing smile. He was in love with everyone at the moment. "I know that,

Natalia. I'll be her eyes. I'll be her eyes from now on. Please. Bring her to me."

Natalia stared up at him for a long moment, then nodded, making up her mind. "Wait here," she said, and dashed back up the stairs.

Elena was moving in a dream. She was going to marry Adam. It hardly seemed possible. It was just too good to be really true. And she was ready. She had on her satin dress, the bodice encrusted with tiny seed pearls, she had on the tiara that made her feel royal, and her veil that felt like a fancy spider web around her head, she had on her tiny satin shoes and was already carrying her bouquet of flowers that spilled delicious scent everywhere. She felt like a princess, a queen, the heroine in a fantasy.

"Like someone in a fairy tale," she murmured to herself.

Natalia stopped beside her and held her hand. "You really love him, don't you?" she said.

"Natalia, if only I could make you understand how I feel. He's just so wonderful, he's…"

Natalia squeezed her hand. "Don't try to explain. The expression on your face tells it all." Then she raised her voice. "Attention, everyone. Would you all please leave me with Elena for a moment? Just go on down and get ready for the big entrance. I'll take care of things here."

There were a few mutterings of protest, but they began to filter out.

"What is it?" Elena asked Natalia, suddenly anxious. "Is something wrong?"

"No, darling. For you, everything has come right."

She pulled Elena to her feet. "Come with me," she whispered. "No questions. Just trust me."

There was only one person in the world Elena trusted more. She let Natalia lead her, carefully negotiating the stairway with her long skirt rustling around her. And suddenly she found herself in Adam's arms.

She gasped, pulling back.

"Don't worry," Natalia told her before she had a chance to protest. "Everything is going to work out fine. Just wait and see."

But Elena wasn't really worried. How could she be? She was with Adam and that was all she could ask for.

"Where are we going?" she asked him, ready for anything.

"Into a wonderland created just for our special day," he told her. "Come with me."

She felt the wave of cool air as he took her out into the snowy but protected courtyard, describing it all to her, making her taste a snowflake on her tongue, showing her how to turn her face up to accept the tiny cold kisses on her warm face. It was magic, a cool, silent world of crystal beauty—and he made her see it all. She laughed, enchanted, and Jeremy joined them, then Fabio.

"Oh, we'd better go in," she said reluctantly when she heard an organ begin to play the wedding march.

"No, we don't have to go in," Adam told her. "Natalia is a genius. She's brought the wedding out to us."

The French doors were suddenly thrown open and their wedding guests began crowding out onto the patio. The minister appeared, and so did the bridesmaids, shivering, but game. Natalia threw a soft shawl around Elena's shoulders as they all sorted themselves out under a rose-covered arbor that stood before the central fountain. Jeremy came to stand beside his father. Gino gave the bride away. And right out in the new snow, the service began.

Elena felt tears welling in her eyes, but the urge to laugh was there, too. She'd never been so happy. She'd never felt such hope. With her friends all around her, with Fabio at her feet, with a whole new family in her life, she brimmed with joy and satisfaction. There was love all around and there were snowflakes in her eyelashes. But, most of all, there was a wonderful man in her heart. And that made her the luckiest woman in the world.

"I do," she said fervently when the time came.

"I do," Adam said as well.

"And now let's all go back inside," Natalia said, "before we freeze."

The others began to surge back in, but the bride and groom lingered in the courtyard for a private moment before rejoining the celebration. Elena melted into Adam's arms and sighed as his lips found hers.

"And they lived happily ever after," Adam murmured, holding her as though she was more precious than life itself.

She laughed. "That's a promise," she agreed. And why not? She was already happier than she'd ever imagined she could be.

* * * * *

*Turn the page to discover
more about*

and

THE ISLAND OF NIROLI

THE ORIGINS OF THE RULES OF THE ROYAL HOUSE OF NIROLI

The Rules of Niroli have dictated the lives – and loves – of the Fierezza family for centuries. In a recent speech the ageing King heralded them as the backbone of the monarchy, provoking speculation that, as unrest begins to bubble away under the surface of the Nirolian people, the Royal House is pulling its traditions even closer. The Rules may be deemed old-fashioned, and even out of touch, but to this day they have never failed the turbulent Fierezza family! As a whole, the Rules are designed to provide unity and continuity for the Island of Niroli. They ensure that the Royal Family conducts itself with dignity – to set an example for its subjects – and keep all the Fierezzas firmly under the control of the monarch.

The Rules

Rule 1: *The ruler must be a moral leader. Any act which brings the Royal House into disrepute will rule a contender out of the succession to the throne.*

Origin: King Alvaro II, who ruled for forty years in the sixteenth century, was a pious and devoted ruler. He added this rule, claiming that he believed that a King of Niroli could have no greater calling than to ensure that he provided a moral compass for the Royal Family and his subjects.

Rule 2: *No member of the Royal House may be joined in marriage without consent of the ruler. Any such union concluded results in exclusion and deprivation of honours and privileges.*

Rule 3: *No marriage is permitted if the interests of Niroli become compromised through the union.*

Origin: Both rule 2 and rule 3 come from the time that the Fierezza dynasty was first formed, when it was considered essential that the King maintained control over his family and whom they married, so that any union would strengthen the illustrious House of Niroli.

Rule 4: *It is not permitted for the ruler of Niroli to marry a person who has previously been divorced.*

Origin: Another ruler, King Benedicio, who was concerned with the morals of the Royal House, considered that it was vital that anybody marrying into it had a spotless reputation. Following Prince Francesco's attempt to marry a divorced European countess with a dubious past in 1793, King Benedicio deemed it necessary to add this rule.

Rule 5: *Marriage between members of the Royal House who are blood relations is forbidden.*

Origin: Many royal houses have suffered from inbreeding, as cousins, and even nieces and uncles, have married each other across the years. King Dominico I declared in 1752 that to keep the Fierezza bloodline strong and healthy, this practice would not be tolerated in the Royal House.

Rule 6: *The ruler directs the education of all members of the Royal House, even when the general care of the children belongs to their parents.*

Origin: In common with most of the ruling houses of Europe, it has always been considered vital that all members of the Fierezza dynasty are brought up with an education which prepares them for their role in the Royal House of Niroli.

Rule 7: *Without the approval or consent of the ruler, no member of the Royal House can make debts over the possibility of payment.*

Origin: A relatively recent addition to the rules, this was added in 1950 when Ricardo Fierezza, an inveterate gambler, found himself in huge financial difficulties after he banked on certain deals coming to fruition that subsequently failed. In order to avoid any more scandals of this nature, the Royal House decided that a rule governing the Fierezzas' financial conduct was in order.

Rule 8: *No member of the Royal House can accept inheritance nor any donation without the consent and approval of the ruler.*

Origin: In the early years of the Fierezzas' rule over Niroli, King Pietro faced a possible usurpation of his throne from his younger brother, Prince Guiseppe, following the latter's acceptance of a huge sum of money from the King of Aragon, Alfonso V. Alfonso wished to gain control of the increasingly wealthy island, already famed for

its trading ports, and was prepared to pay Guiseppe to raise an army and buy the support of any dissident nobles. After his defeat, in 1427, Guiseppe was exiled and King Pietro added this rule to ensure that there could be no repeat of this kind of rebellion ever again.

Rule 9: *The ruler of Niroli must dedicate his life to the Kingdom. Therefore he is not permitted to have a profession.*

Origin: Another rule that is a relatively new addition. As the administrative machine has grown, the Kings of Niroli have found themselves less burdened with the machinations of state. In 1897, King Adriano, a scholarly and shy ruler, consulted over the possibility that he would take up a teaching post. It was decided that the ruler of Niroli must be absolutely dedicated to the island, and that involvement in other professions was undesirable and detrimental to the long-term survival of the monarchy.

Rule 10: *Members of the Royal House must reside in Niroli or in a country approved by the ruler. However the ruler must reside in Niroli.*

Origin: As the Fierezzas' lifestyles became increasingly jet-set, this rule was added as a pre-emptive measure to ensure that the ruler of Niroli would always be able to control the whereabouts of his family. In addition, it was felt that it should be enshrined that the monarch, as part of his dedication to Niroli, must live on the island to provide a focus and a symbol of unity.

A BRIEF HISTORY OF
THE ISLAND OF NIROLI AND
THE ROYAL HOUSE OF NIROLI

Niroli has a colourful and fascinating history filled with ancient rivalries, rebellions and the fight for the ultimate prize – the crown of Niroli.

The Fierezza family has ruled since the Middle Ages and is one of the richest royal families in the world, having founded its fortune on ancient trading routes, thanks to Niroli's prime position to the south of Sicily. Thanks to these links, it has traditionally been seen as the 'Gateway to the East'.

Since the establishment of the Fierezza dynasty, Niroli has thrived as an important European port, situated on major trading routes for spice, wine and perfume. However, while Niroli has prospered, it has a turbulent history right up to the modern day, and after a civil war in 1972 Niroli lost control of the neighbouring island Mont Avellana, which has become a republic. In addition to this, a group of bandits, known as the Viallis, who are ex-Barbary corsairs, formed a resistance against the monarchy. The height of their rebellious activity was in the 1970s and a few remaining Viallis still live in the foothills of the Niroli mountain range.

NIROLI – A TOURIST'S GUIDE

The Island of Niroli

With all it has to offer, who would not be tempted by a holiday on the beautiful island of Niroli? The climate is very agreeable, particularly to the south of the island. There are beautiful sandy beaches, especially around the new development area on the south coast which has been built to attract tourists. In this area you will find luxurious five-star hotels, casinos, restaurants, bars, etc, perfect for a relaxing and sophisticated holiday.

Things to See

The island also has a rich and varied history – don't miss the chance to explore its wonderful Roman ruins. In the north east of the island, there is a Roman amphitheatre where concerts are still performed today, particularly during the festivals celebrating the grape and olive picking seasons. There are also many fine castles to explore. Visitors must see the stunning main town of Niroli. If you enter the port by boat it is particularly impressive, as you see the town sprawling up the hillside in front of you, with the historic old town to your left and the palace just in view. Do wander round the old town and soak up the atmosphere, as well as stopping at the numerous charming shops and exclusive boutiques.

NIROLI – A TOURIST'S GUIDE

Things to Do

For those who enjoy more active pursuits,
there are plenty of opportunities for diving and
swimming, then afterwards, relaxing in the
wonderful spa and beauty treatment area on the
east coast. To the west of the island you can
walk and climb in the mountains and take in the
stunning views across the Mediterranean. The
central part of the island is devoted mainly to
agriculture, with the vineyards extending to the
rolling foothills of the mountains. There are also
olive groves, orchards and livestock and Niroli
is deservedly famous for its fine olive oil and
wonderful wines.

NIROLI – ISLAND PRODUCE

Niroli is a sun-drenched and idyllic Mediterranean isle. Thanks to the now-extinct volcanoes, Nirolians enjoy lush and fertile conditions in which to grow a wonderful range of produce, famed the world over, and are surrounded by an abundant and generous sea which provides wonderful local fare.

Oranges
Niroli is famous for its orange groves of Cattina, which produce a particularly sweet-flavoured fruit. Oil of Niroli is extracted from the orange skins. Niroli has a floral, citrussy, sweet and exotic scent, which is used to make perfume, aromatherapy oil and health and beauty products; it has special healing, rejuvenating, soothing and restorative properties which make it especially popular for relaxation and anti-ageing treatments and scar reduction therapy at the Santa Fiera Spa, which has an international reputation for the excellence of its products.

Olives

Green olive trees flourish on the rocky limestone soil in the fertile Cattina Valley. The fruit is prized by cooks, and the island exports olives whole, pitted, stuffed and marinated.

Niroli Virgin Olive and Orange Oil is a delicacy; infused with the zest of local oranges, it is particularly delicious when drizzled over fish, seafood, chicken, asparagus or pasta, and you can sample all of these dishes in Niroli's excellent array of restaurants.

Grapes

The Niroli vines produce the queen of white grapes. Cultivated since Roman times on the slopes of the Cattina Valley, and ripened by summer sun and storms, these grapes are harvested to make Porto Castellante Bianco, a dry white wine with a crisp, citrussy bouquet, which makes an especially good accompaniment to fish dishes.

Marine life

The seas around the island of Niroli are fertile fishing grounds, filled with bass, bream, tuna, red snapper, squid, shrimp and scallops. The fishing fleet goes out daily to catch the local sea's fine bounty. Natives and tourists alike savour these catches and the island's speciality dish of red mullet, which is marinated in Niroli Virgin Olive and Orange Oil, then lightly grilled.

The Santa Fiera Spa also makes excellent use

of an abundance of marine algae in its skin and
beauty treatments.

Volcanic Mud

The volcanoes on Niroli are now extinct, but the
area around them is still a rich source of volcanic
mud, which is a mixture of rainwater and volcanic
ash formed at the time of eruption.

The Santa Fiera Spa specialises in volcanic mud
baths and masks as health and beauty treatments,
which are reported to rejuvenate and revitalise the
skin, drawing women from across the globe keen
to take advantage of its miraculous properties!

MORE ABOUT THE AUTHOR

RAYE MORGAN

Raye Morgan has been writing romances for years – and fostering romance in her own family at the same time. Current score: two boys married, two more to go. Raye has published over seventy romances, and claims to have many more waiting in the wings. She still lives in Southern California, with her husband and whichever son happens to be staying at home at the moment. When not writing, she can be found feverishly working on family genealogy and scrapbooking. So many pictures – so little time!

RAYE MORGAN
QUESTIONS & ANSWERS

Did you enjoy the experience of writing about Niroli?

Writing a story set in Niroli was like taking a vacation at a wonderful island resort – only the experience wasn't limited to interacting with a few waiters and tourist staffers – instead, I got to stay with real locals and get to know the area well. I printed out pictures of my conception of what the island would be like and had them up all over the walls, so that every time I looked up, my feeling of being in Niroli was reinforced.

Would you like to visit Niroli?

I already have, but I would go again in a heartbeat!

Which of the 'Rules of Niroli' would you least like to abide by?

I'm afraid I wouldn't like any of them very much. Though I'm basically a boring, stay-inside-the-lines sort of person, arbitrary rules of behaviour always rub me the wrong way.

How did you find writing as part of a continuity?

I loved writing as part of a continuity. It's so much fun knowing your story is a part of an entire community where everyone's path intersects everyone else's. I loved reading all the stories and catching references to people from the other books.

When you are writing, what is your typical day?

Lots of coffee, lots of procrastination, snacks, checking the internet – and then finally getting down to business and writing and rewriting the rest of the day away.

Where do you find the inspiration that shapes your characters?

I love to people-watch, especially in cafés or at the beach. Watching people interact and dreaming about what their lives might possibly be like always opens up so many possibilities.

What, in your opinion, makes a great hero?

For me, the best heroes are solid, manly guys with a touch of wildness in their souls. They just need a little love to tame them. A sense of humour certainly helps, an appreciation for what makes a woman special, and a deep, abiding – though sometimes temporarily denied – need for intimacy.

Tell us about the project you're working on at the moment.

I've just finished a Boss and Baby book which will be out soon, but I've had so much fun doing the last couple of stories with royal themes, I'm working on an idea for a royal series of my own. Wish me luck!

THE ROYAL HOUSE OF NIROLI

Each month The Royal House of Niroli brings you an exciting new story in the search for the true Nirolian king. Eight heirs, eight loves, eight fantastic stories!

Time after time the Fierezza descendants have chosen love over their right to rule Niroli. But one man has always put duty first. Now he is about to complete his destiny...

The heat off the runway echoed in waves, the crowd gathered, shuffling, whispering, jostling, waiting. As the door opened silence descended. Then, behind a row of bodyguards, he appeared. And a roar rippled through the throng.

He was no ordinary leader – he was their king, their ruler, their protector. And he was there not to greet them, but to say his final goodbye. His people drank in the moment. Some men bowed their heads in respect, whilst the women could barely take their eyes from him. His skin glowed a honeyed gold from days out in the desert and the collar of his sharp white shirt grazed the shadow of dark hair on his neck. The stubble that ran up over his chiselled jaw was the only tell-tale sign of the sleepless nights he had spent agonising his fate. The exquisite cut of his feather-light cashmere suit emphasised the broadness of his shoulders and the long length of his legs as he strode out across the tarmac towards the plane. He was leaving them, but he would carry a piece of this land with him in his heart forever.

As the engines of the aircraft revved into gear, he turned on the steps to take one last glance at his country. He looked out at the crowd below him. A sight he would remember for his lifetime. He gave a final salute, the sound of the cheers and cries was deafening. And then he was gone.

And so the true ruler of Niroli makes his way to the small island that will become his future. Discover how the royal house react to this magnificent man and his claim to the throne of Niroli in

A ROYAL BRIDE AT THE SHEIKH'S COMMAND,

the exciting conclusion to
The Royal House of Niroli.

Read on for an exclusive extract from the thrilling final instalment!

A ROYAL BRIDE AT THE SHEIKH'S COMMAND

SHE was in total shock.

She needed very badly to sit down, but of course she couldn't. For one thing she was still in the Royal Presence Chamber, and, whilst she was a modern go-getting woman, her Nirolian ancestry within her reminded her that she was alone in the presence of Niroli's King.

And for another… Well, she told herself grimly, the king wasn't going to welcome seeing any kind of weakness being shown by the bride he had selected for this newly discovered heir. So newly discovered, in fact, that she, the bride-to-be in question, had been sworn to absolute secrecy about the whole thing.

It was of course a story that would attract every member of the paparazzi like blood in the water attracted sharks, and one that could be just as potentially perilous to anyone who obstructed King Giorgio's plans. She had just learned that these plans required her, as a dutiful subject, to marry this Prince Kadir Zafar, the King's previously 'secret' illegitimate son, for the sake of the island she loved so passionately.

CHAPTER ONE

Venice

SHE might be passionately attached to Niroli, but there
was no doubt that Venice had a very special place in her
heart, Natalia acknowledged, lifting her hand to try to
stop the breeze from playing with the heavy weight of
her thick dark curls. She was waiting for the water taxi
to take her to her destination, and was totally oblivious
to the admiring male looks she was attracting. When one
man proved bold enough to murmur, *'Bella, bella,'* ca-
ressingly as he stopped to stand and stare openly at her,
she couldn't help but laugh, her marine blue eyes sparkling with the rich colour of the lido in the sunshine. Just
having her sombre mood lightened for a few seconds
was a much needed relief at the moment.

It was all very well having sleepless nights and
worrying herself half a stone thinner over whether or not
she had made the right decision, but what she ought to
be asking herself surely was why on earth had she ever
agreed to do it in the first place.

The water taxi arrived and she picked up her small weekend bag and stepped into the taxi with ease and elegance. She was a tall woman of close to six feet who wore her height with calm pride.

'Via Venetii? The Buchesetti Spa Hotel,' she asked the *vaporetto* driver.

'*Sì,*' he agreed, with open admiration in his gaze.

The tranquil ride to her destination made Natalia reflect ruefully on the uncomfortable speed with which the direction of her life had suddenly changed. Increasingly she was waking up in the morning feeling as though she had stepped on board a train that had then suddenly picked up speed to such an extent that she was beginning to feel that it was running away with her.

So why had she allowed it to happen in the first place? After all no one had forced her.

No? When your king appealed to you personally for your help to save the future of your country, a country you loved, you didn't just turn round and say no, did you? At least not if you were a Carini.

The trouble was that, since she had said yes, the list of reasons why in her own interests she would have been better off saying no had begun to grow by the day.

'Via Venetii,' the *vaporetto* driver pointed out to her, interrupting her thoughts. 'The hotel, she is not far now. Is a very beautiful hotel. You go there before?'

'Yes,' Natalia told him. She could see from the expression on his face that the answer had sounded more curt than she had intended. But how could she explain to him how she felt about the fact that she had been obliged to sell her beloved spa hotel on Niroli to this one in Venice?

True, the choice of whom she should sell to had been her own. True, too, that she knew that the new owners, Maya and Howard, would uphold her own high standards, now that they had officially added her spa to their portfolio, but that still did not mean that she was not allowed to grieve for her much cherished and loved 'baby', did it?

So why give it up in the first place? Why give up the life she had worked so hard to build for herself to enter into an arranged marriage of state? So that she could be a princess? Natalia almost laughed out loud, the white flash of her even white teeth contrasting with the full warmth of her soft red lips making the driver of the *vaporetto* sigh in a way that caused Natalia to look away to conceal her amusement.

At twenty-nine she had had ample time to get used to her effect on the opposite sex.

To get used to her effect on the opposite sex, but never to fall in love. And now with her forthcoming marriage to the newly discovered heir to the Nirolian throne she was giving up the chance to do so for ever, wasn't she? After all, she wasn't foolish enough to think that a marriage arranged between two strangers by a king whose only thought was to secure the future of his kingdom could by some miracle turn into a passionately intense and lifelong love affair, was she? Not when she had never, ever fallen in love; not when her sole reason for agreeing to this marriage had been her passionate love, not for a man, but for a country, *her* country, just as her husband-to-be's desire was directed towards the throne of Niroli and not towards her. Could it work? Was she as mad as she was beginning to think to have agreed to marry Prince Kadir just so that she would be there at his side to ensure that he ruled her beloved country with wisdom and love? If only there were someone she could turn to for advice, but there wasn't. The king had forbidden her to discuss the matter with anyone.

The elegant and exclusive spa hotel that was her destination had its own landing stage. As she saw it approaching Natalia turned to pick up her bag. As she did so a man striding impatiently across the small square to the side of the hotel caught her eye, as much for any other reason as for his height. At almost six feet herself, she was appreciative of the visual impact of men who were taller than her, and this man was certainly that, taller, and broad shouldered, with surprisingly hard-packed muscles, too, for a man who looked as though he was closer to forty than thirty. Thick dark hair that just brushed the collar of his jacket gleamed with good health under the brilliant sunlight. His skin was warmly olive and although he was too far away for Natalia to see the colour of his eyes she could see the hard, precision hewn perfection of his facial bone structure with its high cheekbones and strong jaw. Here was a man, she acknowledged.

As though by some alchemic means he had somehow sensed her interest and paused, turning his head to look directly at her. She still could not see the colour of his eyes, but she could see that he was even more stunningly handsome face on than he had been in profile. It had to be the sun that was making her feel slightly dizzy and not the fact that he was looking at her... Had been looking at her, she recognised to her relief as he turned away and resumed his progress across the square. As the *vaporetto* pulled into the landing stage she admitted to herself that her brief interest in this man was not the wisest of things in a woman soon to enter into a dynastic marriage. How was she going to go on in that marriage if she was experiencing sexual desire for another man now? Sexual desire? That was ridiculous. She had simply been looking at him, that was all, and anyway he had gone now, and she was hardly likely to ever see him again, was she?

If you've missed any of the volumes in *The Royal House of Niroli* collection, you can have them delivered straight to your door:

Book Title/Author	ISBN & Price	Quantity
1. *The Future King's Pregnant Mistress* Penny Jordan	978 0263 85872 3 £2.99	
2. *Surgeon Prince, Ordinary Wife* Melanie Milburne	978 0263 85873 0 £2.99	
3. *Bought by the Billionaire Prince* Carol Marinelli	978 0263 85874 7 £2.99	
4. *The Tycoon's Princess Bride* Natasha Oakley	978 0263 85875 4 £2.99	
5. *Expecting His Royal Baby* Susan Stephens	978 0263 85876 1 £2.99	
6. *The Prince's Forbidden Virgin* Robyn Donald	978 0263 85877 8 £2.99	
7. *Bride by Royal Appointment* Raye Morgan	978 0263 85878 5 £2.99	
8. *A Royal Bride at the Sheikh's Command* Penny Jordan	978 0263 85879 2 £2.99	

Please add 99p postage & packing per book
DELIVERY TO UK ONLY

Post to: End Page Offer, PO Box 1780, Croydon, CR9 3UH

E-mail: customer.relations@hmb.co.uk

Please ensure that you include full postal address details.
Please pay by cheque or postal order (payable to Reader Service).
Prices and availability subject to change without notice.

Order online at: www.millsandboon.co.uk

Allow 28 days for delivery.

THE ROYAL HOUSE OF NIROLI

...International affairs, seduction and passion guaranteed

Volume 1 – July 2007
The Future King's Pregnant Mistress by Penny Jordan

Volume 2 – August 2007
Surgeon Prince, Ordinary Wife by Melanie Milburne

Volume 3 – September 2007
Bought by the Billionaire Prince by Carol Marinelli

Volume 4 – October 2007
The Tycoon's Princess Bride by Natasha Oakley

8 volumes in all to collect!

THE ROYAL HOUSE OF NIROLI

*...International affairs, seduction
and passion guaranteed*

Volume 5 – November 2007
Expecting His Royal Baby by Susan Stephens

Volume 6 – December 2007
The Prince's Forbidden Virgin by Robyn Donald

Volume 7 – January 2008
Bride by Royal Appointment by Raye Morgan

Volume 8 – February 2008
A Royal Bride at the Sheikh's Command by Penny Jordan

8 volumes in all to collect!

THE ROYAL HOUSE OF NIROLI

...*International affairs, seduction and passion guaranteed*

VOLUME EIGHT

A Royal Bride at the Sheikh's Command by Penny Jordan

Sheikh Kadir: the ruler of an eastern kingdom in which his every word is obeyed and every gesture revered. And he's also the last heir to Niroli's throne. Now Kadir is called upon to leave his desert people and seek welcome from his new subjects...and find himself a queen!

Natalia Carini is dedicated to running Niroli's luxurious spa. She loves her island home and to her, Sheikh Kadir is an invader and a thief. He's clearly used to taking what he wants, when he wants! He's already helped himself to Niroli and now he's demanding her as his bride!

To be Kadir's wife and Niroli's queen are challenges Natalia can handle... But to be bedded by a barbarian excites her more than she's ever known...

Available 1st February 2008

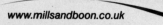